Alien Wreck
Live Alien Contact: Book One
Copyright © 2025 Leah Cutter
All rights reserved
Published by Knotted Road Press
www.KnottedRoadPress.com
ISBN: 978-1-64470-461-5

Cover Art:
ID 126231620 | Spaceship © Philcold | Dreamstime.com

Cover and interior design copyright © 2025 Knotted Road Press

Reviews

It's true. Reviews help me sell more books. If you've enjoyed this story, please consider leaving a review of it on your favorite site.

Come someplace new...

Do you enjoy exploring strange new worlds, new cultures, new people?

Journey into the various lands envisioned by Leah R Cutter.

Sign up for my newsletter and I'll start you on your travels with a free copy of my book, *The Island Sampler.*

http://www.LeahCutter.com/newsletter/

ALSO BY LEAH R CUTTER

Science Fiction

Live Alien Contact

Alien Wreck

Alien Codex

Alien Encounter

Alien War

The Long Run

Project Nemesis

Project Nyx

Project Tisiphone

Project Persephone

War of the Allied Worlds

The Complete Labors of Darius Linard

Huli Intergalactic: Science/Space Fantasy

Origins

The Strawberry Girl

Urban/Contemporary Fantasy Series

The Witch's Progress

Circle of Air

Circle of Fire

ALIEN WRECK

LIVE ALIEN CONTACT
BOOK 1

LEAH R CUTTER

KNOTTED ROAD PRESS

ONE

Rosey took one last walk all the way around the latest speedship she'd built. She'd designed it with sleek lines, though aerodynamics really didn't matter when it came to spaceships.

However, this was a racing ship. Messing with your opponents' perceptions, getting inside their heads, was part of the race.

If you looked slick, fast, and deadly, your opponents would unconsciously fear you. It might give you that very slight edge that you needed to win.

This speedship had a stereotypical cylindrical rocket shape and length, about sixteen feet long. The front end narrowed down to a needle-sharp point. The middle held a small cockpit, big enough for a single person to be strapped into, sitting up, their legs stretched out. A transparent bubble covered the top of the cockpit, just above the pilot's head, so that she could see out if she wanted to. Most pilots didn't care, as they were dependent on the display projected inside their helmet as well as on their dashboard.

Rosey had always wanted to be able to see out when she'd

raced, so unless specified otherwise in the contract, she included the ability to view the space around the racer through their eyes and not just relying on the computer displays.

A large red ring encircled the rear of the ship, connected to the body with a series of black S-shaped fan blades. She'd designed them so that they'd looked as though they were in motion, an imaginary wind blowing through them. The ring contained most of the ship's pulsers and gyros. Stubby red wings along the sides of the ship's body worked in concert with the pulsers, giving the ship a better turning radius.

A specialized porcelain alloy covered the ship, which gave it a pretty gray sheen, like burnished steel. As this was for a client Rosey liked, she'd used a factory standard color, though personally, she would have gone for something flashier.

In certain circles, racers still talked of the shimmering pink monstrosity that Rosey had built for a client who'd been an asshole.

He'd won his race, of course. Rosey's sense of personal pride wouldn't allow her to build a shoddy speedship.

However, that contract hadn't specified a color for the ship, so Rosey had gotten...*creative*. The exterior was hot pink and sparkling. Plush red-velvet covered the pilot's chair, pink shag-carpet enveloped the cockpit, and purple- and gold-colored paisleys decorated every other surface. In addition, she'd done a custom job on the lighting scheme for the controls, so that they continually cycled from cool blue up to garish orange and back again.

The asshole couldn't merely paint the exterior either, not without ruining the alloy Rosey had used. He'd have to completely reskin the speedship.

Eventually the asshole did, but he never won another race with that ship once he'd changed the color.

His opponents all knew he had fear. And they took advantage of that.

As Rosey completed her inspection of her latest creation, a call came through her bonephone. It was hardwired into her collarbone, allowing her to communicate both subvocally as well as read texts sent via the contact she wore on her right eye.

Jamaal had another ship he wanted her to go investigate.

Rosey couldn't help but roll her eyes. She let the call go through to her automated answering system.

"Aren't you going to respond to that?"

Though the words came through the bonephone, and she still heard them as if they'd been spoken out loud.

They came from Dennis, the AI who ran her starship, and in many ways, her life.

"I'll talk with Jamaal later," Rosey promised. And she would. Jamaal was someone she'd consider a friend, not a client or even a prospect. He was a trader of sorts: if you had a need, he generally had a friend who knew someone who knew someone who could fix you up.

For a fee, of course.

"But it might be important," Dennis said.

"It's just about his latest find," Rosey said as she whistled a ladder over to her.

Jamaal was obsessed with finding an alien spaceship. On planets, people searched for sentient oceans, ghosts, or even Bigfoot. In space, that same type of person searched for aliens. With about the same amount of luck.

Sure, Humans had run across two planets that contained the remains of alien civilizations. First they'd found evidence of the Harmaiz, a tall, skeletal, insect-like being on the planet Zonami. Later, they'd found the Atoylee, a more plant-based alien likened to sunflowers, on the planet Niani.

No one had yet to meet an actual, living alien.

Whatever Jamaal had thought he'd found, it wasn't alive and kicking, and so it could wait.

The speedship rested on risers in Rosey's drydock workshop. The shop was big enough to hold four ships with enough room to work around them, as well as Rosey's fabrication facility and engine station. While she could build speedship engines from scratch, the racing circuit rules were persnickety about materials and design. Instead of hassling with them, she ordered top-of-the=line pre-built cores, then adjusted everything she could, eking out every last ounce of speed and control while staying within the guidelines.

The back of Rosey's workshop connected to the space station *Lorenzo*, while the front of it had a specialized airlock that she used for direct access to space. It was only big enough for one speedship at a time, though Rosey had thought about widening it more than once.

Rosey's personal quarters were aboard her own starship. The workshop, just on its own, was bigger than most people's apartments on the space station. Since Rosey traveled a lot, she preferred to take her home with her. The additional space didn't hurt either.

As Rosey climbed the ladder to get into the cockpit of her latest speedship, Dennis spoke up again. "What are you doing?"

"Gotta test this ship," Rosey said, trying to sound reasonable. "It's in the contract."

The expressive sigh from Dennis made her grin. She could reprogram him to be less of a nag, but where was the fun in that?

"Tell me that you at least are wearing your stretchsuit," came Dennis's long suffering reply.

"Yes, Mother, I am," Rosey said. Her stretchsuit was custom made, of course. The fabric stretched over her body tightly, showing off the muscles she'd maintained by doing so much manual labor and martial arts, even though she was in her mid-fifties. The color was a deep, rich, and frankly, rosy red. Over the chest were her initials, embroidered in white—RDV —Rosey De Vries.

The name for a stretchsuit didn't necessarily come from the stretchy material, but from the fact that a stretchsuit was supposed to protect you in case of an accident in space, stretching out your life so that you could survive long enough for someone to rescue you. In a standard stretchsuit, you could technically survive in pure space for up to twenty minutes, but Rosey never liked to push it.

A backpack came built into the suit. It contained air and heat elements. It was about two inches thick and covered her entire back. Rosey's ships always had extra air cylinders and batteries built into the cockpit, on either side of the pilot's chair, that could be attached to a stretchsuit and thereby extend that twenty minutes of life substantially.

The backpack also contained the helmet that Rosey activated, covering her head and sealing the suit. She kept her gray curls short so they would stay out of the way of the helmet. Not spacer-short: the people who lived in actual EVA suits tended to shave their heads down to stubble. She kept hers long enough that she had hair she could actually run her fingers through, maybe even put gel in when she was feeling feisty, but short enough to not get in the way.

Though the contract specified exact dimensions for the cockpit and the pilot's chair, Rosey always made the chairs slightly adjustable, so that when the speedship had finished its racing career, it could be sold and the next buyer didn't have to be the exact same height as the original pilot Or have to rip out the pilot's seat and replace it.

Plus, that way, she could always take the ships out for one final test run, adjusting the seat forward. She was five seven, and all her height was in her torso like a guy, not her legs.

Rosey ran through the initial flight checklist, never skimping corners on that.

Sometimes, you could rush through a checklist. Particularly in an emergency, when you needed to get off planet before some angry local sheriff came after you. (Not that she'd ever had any experience with that. No, really. Those stories were just that. Made-up tales.)

However, the initial flight of any ship was not the time.

This particular speedship had been exposed to pure space, more than once, to ensure that it was airtight. Rosey wasn't worried about it suddenly springing a leak, losing pressure, or whatnot. Her checklist was as much superstition as anything else.

Finally, Rosey was ready. She lightly touched the pulsers to raise the ship up, off the risers, then pointed its nose toward the airlock and through the first set of doors.

As she waited for the pressure to equalize and the second set of doors to open, she set up the obstacle course she wanted to race on the ship's computer.

All Rosey did was give the course parameters, such as two straightaways, two sets of sharp curves, a turnaround midway, and a slalom section.

The computer then randomly generated the course for her to follow, adding in two random elements.

She could have had the computer completely generate the entire course, or she could have specified everything.

For official races, a special computer created the virtual

course nanoseconds before the race began, ensuring that each courses was different and that no one had the opportunity to learn the course beforehand.

The exterior doors of her workshop opened as the display in the cockpit showed the start of the course.

A second ship appeared beside hers on her display.

"Really, Dennis?" Rosey asked with an exaggerated sigh.

"Aren't you the one who always says test everything? Don't merely rely on simulations?" Dennis replied smugly.

"Fine," Rosey said with an eyeroll.

"We could make it interesting, you know. Spice it up with a bet," Dennis said.

"You know I don't bet on winning," Rosey said. If too many credits were involved, she might be tempted to cut corners and fly an unsafe race.

Well, cut more corners than necessary.

"You're the boss," Dennis said, sounding suspiciously cheerful.

What did that sneaky AI of hers have planned?

Rosey just grinned as she felt her heart rate accelerate.

"All right then. Let's race."

Of course, Dennis was first across the starting line when the lights on her display all shone GO.

He would have that edge on her, his artificial reflexes more finely tuned. In many ways, he represented youth and skill.

Whereas all Rosey had was old age and treachery.

She'd just have to make do with those.

The slalom portion was the first hazard on the race course, and appeared immediately after the initial straightaway. As

Rosey hadn't specified, this one was done as a series of six markers, set high and low, not side to side.

The pilot's yoke turned the ship, as well as rasing and lowering its nose. Buttons under Rosey's fingers controlled gyros and thrusters, while her feet managed general speed and deceleration.

Though Dennis had gotten a two-second head start, Rosey caught up with him on the first set of slalom markers. She used the perfect combination of thrust and abrupt deceleration to get her up above the marker, then headed back down again.

Mind you, she might only have a fraction of an inch between the belly of her ship and the marker. But as it was just a point on the course set by the computer, not an actual physical buoy, so that sort of skimming was legal.

At the next marker, she pulled back hard on the yoke, thrusters at max, then cut everything so she didn't level out, but instead, hinged. That sent her down the far side of the marker quickly, her nose still slightly ahead of the ship racing beside her.

The next marker was set further out, and Rosey let Dennis pull ahead of her. She didn't accelerate abruptly, but steadily, riding up over the next marker like surfing a wave, up and down gradually.

It wasn't until the last marker that she pulled out all the stops, hinging up and over it as she had the first couple of slalom markers.

Dennis was caught by surprise, which was the point. She left him behind her as they entered into the first of the sharp curves.

The speedship shimmied as she turned, the rear end pivoting out slightly, as she'd anticipated. She rode that inertia and went into the next curve with fractions of an inch to spare, just clearing the markers.

This time, Dennis caught onto her tricks quickly, and once they were through the curves, they were nose and nose again on another straightaway section, one of the two random bits that the computer had added, just before the midway turn.

As it wasn't a real ship beside her, Rosey may have possibly drifted a slight bit closer. Just enough to get Dennis to back away. And slow down.

She grinned when he growled at her. Those automatic systems of his were both an advantage as well as a disadvantage. Any new behavior would spark an automated response until he learned better.

She could probably slow him down by getting too close at least once more before those systems of his figured it out. The trick wouldn't work a third time.

The midway turn was a point that separated the amateurs from the pros. How much you slowed down, how quickly you could overcome your forward momentum, were as much pilot skill as mechanical ability.

Rosey had something special planned for this one. Instead of trying to turn sideways and go around the marker on a single plane, she dove down, going under it, then yanked back hard enough on her yoke to pull her up abruptly on the other side.

She flew over the top of the turnaround point upside down, leaving behind a grumbling Dennis, who'd flown the safer route, going around it instead.

The third straightaway led out of the midpoint turn, giving Dennis a chance to almost catch up.

Almost.

Another slalom course showed up next, the second random

element generated by the computer. This one was a side-to-side hazard.

Dennis appeared to have caught on to Rosey's tricks by now, and was shaving the distance he used going around the markers, bringing the nose of his ship closer to hers, particularly as they made their way through the last straightaway.

Then it was the final set of sharp curves. Rosey had hoped that this would be the case. She drifted again as she had in the first set, allowing her rear end to shimmy out slightly.

Dennis was prepared for that, giving her space, but not slowing down.

Then Rosey drifted further out.

Dennis had no choice but to pull away as Rosey slammed everything home.

During the last curve, Rosey didn't drift in the slightest, keeping everything tight, giving her that slight advantage as they raced down the final section, back toward the finish line that the computer had set up a good distance from the space station, giving her time to slow down and not run into anything.

Rosey's ship passed across the line first, at least a full half second before Dennis.

"You're not supposed to be able to do that," were the sour words from Dennis when they'd finished. "How can you judge the markers so accurately? You were closer to the buoy markers than you should have been able to get. You should have gone through them, or brushed them, or something."

Rosey just laughed. "Experience," she told him.

"But I have experience," Dennis whined. "I've been following you and your races for years."

"All you have is programming," Rosey said, sobering. "You don't have instinct."

The long-suffering sigh from Dennis told her everything. It was an argument they'd have before, that he should be able to be as good as the best of the Human pilots given all his processing and skills.

However, he didn't have instinct. He couldn't just *know* where a marker was, intuitively, and how a ship would respond, when pushed to its limits.

It was what had won Rosey so many medals and races, reaching the top level of her class of speedship, before she'd left the circuit.

As Rosey drifted toward her airlock, another call from Jamaal came through her bonephone.

She let it go to her answering system again, but she promised herself that she'd call him back as soon as she got back to the station.

She didn't have to personally deliver this speedship, so she could use a company to send it to her client. Plus, she had over a month before the next speedship needed to be completed. Plenty of time to go on whatever wild goose chase Jamaal had in mind.

Because she was pretty certain that whatever Jamaal thought he had found, it wouldn't be truly alien.

Sure, there were live aliens out there. Somewhere. However, the chances of finding them were smaller than Dennis winning a race against her.

TWO

Jamaal gracefully slid his hands from his left side to in front of his torso, bringing them down with a percussive blow. Then he moved his right arm, flowing until the next strike, which he ended with a hard jerk again.

There were many ways to go through the Tai Chi form that he preferred, a Yang variation with eighty-eight moves. Sometimes he went through the entire form so slowly it took three-quarters of an hour to complete. Other times, he sped through the poses so that it took merely twelve minutes. Then there were times like this morning, when he smoothly went through all the transitional movements while exaggerating every strike, blow, or kick, to bring home the very martial application of this form.

Flow. Rise up. **Break an arm.** *Step. Flow.* **Jab eyes or windpipe.** *Turn. Grab.* **Throw.**

Jamaal practiced in his dedicated workout room. Every square foot of livable habitat on the *Lorenzo* space station was at a premium, but Jamaal had enough money that he could afford the extra space, such as his workout room, his aeroponics room, and his salon, located at the front of his suite, where he entertained guests and clients, in addition to the usual sleeping and eating rooms that everyone had.

Mirrors covered all four walls of the workout room, so Jamaal could study his form from every angle. In front of the mirrors were racks for weights and a few exercise machines. A sanitizing closet sat in the far corner, giving Jamaal the freedom to work out at any time and not have to worry about traipsing through his rooms in a disheveled state.

In the opposite corner stood a rack for the various weapons that Jamaal trained with: sticks, canes, short and long staffs, as well as half a dozen practice swords. Next to that was a locked case, secured with the best biometrics credits could buy. It wasn't very big, maybe three feet in all dimensions. It held all of the *other* weapons Jamaal had expertise in: lasers, projectile weapons, garrotes, knives, and shuriken. Most of which were legal in this system, but certainly not in all.

Of course, Jamaal wore his matte black sharkskin armor. He'd spent too many years working as an assassin for the Emperor, making too many potential enemies, to ever go without it.

Like a stretchsuit, the sharkskin armor tightly covered his body. It was strong enough to withstand most knives. A needle-laser would pierce it, but larger beam particles would be scattered by it. Only prolonged contact with one of those would cut through the armor.

And if Jamaal wasn't moving, he was already dead.

Jamaal caught sight of himself as he turned. He stood just a hair over six feet tall, thin and lithe. His "profession" as it were, when he'd been working for the Emperor, had required more stealth than muscles, though he had those as well. His dark brown skin extended smoothly from the short sleeves of the sharkskin armor. He kept his kinky brown hair shaved short—never give an opponent something to grab. Harkeen, Jamaal's lover, always claimed that Jamaal's dark eyes were soulful, something that Jamaal worked hard to hide from everyone else. Jamaal's forehead was broad, as was his nose, melting across his face. His lips, something he privately considered his best feature, were thick and wide, and according to Harkeen, very kissable.

For now, Jamaal kept those lips in a firm line, his face bland and forgettable, as he continued moving through the form.

It was still odd for him to see his arms as he worked. Though it had been five years since he'd plied his trade for the Emperor, he'd worn full sharkskin armor until just recently. Harkeen had finally persuaded him to put on a lighter suit, one that stopped just before his elbows and knees, retiring the suit that had completely covered his arms and legs.

Maybe in a year or two he'd transition to just body armor, something that merely protected his torso.

He couldn't imagine ever going without some sort of armor. No matter how much Harkeen teased him about being paranoid.

Being paranoid had saved Jamaal's life more than once. So he wore his armor at all times, except for those few, very special occasions with Harkeen.

Finally, Jamaal finished his form. Though he wasn't too sweaty, he still stepped into the sanitizing closet, the sonic vibrations whisking away all traces of his exertions.

Refreshed, Jamaal exited the closet and put back on the bright orange robes that covered him from neck to ankle, as well as all the way down to his wrists. Gold rope embroidery decorated the standing red collar. No one except Harkeen knew that the thread was reinforced with spidersilk, strong enough to withstand most knives or piercing weapons. Same with the embroidery around Jamaal's cuffs, along the base of the flowing robe, as well as the front panel that acted as backing for the brilliant yellow knots and loops that drew the robe tight across Jamaal's chest.

No one could see the sharkskin armor. Possibly only a handful of Jamaal's acquaintances even knew he wore it, and most of them were enemies.

Jamaal felt his face change, and he embraced the wide grin he now saw in the mirror.

Gone was the serious Jamaal, the one who could hide and blend in with a crowd. Who knew more ways to disarm or kill a person than most. Who generally considered violence first, not as an alternative.

Out came Jamaal the trader, the gregarious, happy one. The one who drew attention to himself deliberately. The one who knew everybody, or had a cousin or a friend who did.

The one who actually had fun.

Part of why Jamaal had retired from his work for the Emperor had been because of this persona. What did it say about him if the "real" him hated his life, while this person he became, this cover identity, enjoyed it?

He told himself that he hadn't retired because he'd been getting old. Forty-eight wasn't old.

Now fifty, that might be old, or so he'd teased Harkeen at his last birthday when he'd passed that mark.

Jamaal sauntered out of the room, sending yet a third message to Rosey. He really needed her to go and look at the new ship that had been found *now*. Before the Kollective arranged for it to "disappear," as it had the ones prior to this.

Of course, various governments as well as some incredibly wealthy private individuals offered huge prizes to those who found the first real, live aliens. Jamaal didn't care about the money.

He just wanted to be first.

Rosey finally answered, and they arranged to meet in an hour, over on her starship, *The Roadrunner*.

Jamaal hurried to his kitchen, picking up a container of fresh focaccia, spiced with the seven types of oregano that he grew in his aeroponics unit, along with a small container of the best synthetic olive oil money could buy, also heavily spiced.

He could afford actual olive oil, grown on Earth, but Rosey didn't appreciate it as much as the bread.

His broad steps swirled the robes around his feet as Jamaal walked briskly to a nearby shared flitter. Rosey lived all the way around on the other side of *Lorenzo*. At this time of day, when it felt as though most of the eighteen million inhabitants were awake and in the crowded corridors of the space station, it was quicker to fly around the exterior of the space station rather than take the automated trains or walkways that went through the diameter.

While the pre-programmed flitter darted around the space station, Jamaal considered his best approach with Rosey.

She wasn't interested in the mystery of the aliens. Either Humans would find live ones (and they'd be in trouble) or the aliens would find Humans (and the Humans would be in trouble). Until then, she was content to let the mystery remain a mystery.

Jamaal knew too much about the inner workings of the three Human governments that ruled known space to believe that there had been live alien contact. Not yet. No matter how many rumors he heard, or back-channel chatter. No government could ever keep a secret like that.

First there was the Kollective, the group closest to Earth,

with ninety of the three hundred settled planets pledging their allegiance. The Kollective was the most conservative of all the governments. Harkeen called them stodgy. Then again, Harkeen sometimes called *Jamaal* stodgy, for wearing the same sorts of outfits and liking the same sorts of food all the time.

Then there was the Empire, ruled by Emperor Ogawa and the Empress Consort. They accounted for one hundred and nine of the planets, and ruled as a benevolent dictatorship, or at least that was what all the press releases said.

As Jamaal had worked for the Emperor for over twenty years, he knew that on some worlds the *dictator* aspect was more prevalent than the *benevolent* part. Then again, that was mostly due to the nature of the government on those worlds, rather than rules enforced by the court.

Last and certainly least was the Alliance of Allied Worlds, generally referred to as just the Allied Worlds. Though a significant number of planets were under their umbrella, their government, what little of it existed, was more of a politely armed society than a place of commerce. Sure, it was possible to get rich out in the outskirts. You were more likely to get stabbed, shot, kidnapped, or murdered for your trouble. Possibly all of the above. And what law enforcement existed was extremely corrupt.

The latest alien ship—and Jamaal really did think this one was of alien manufacture, and not Human made, unlike the last two ships he'd sent Rosey to investigate—had been found on the outskirts of Allied World territory.

How this one had fallen under Kollective "protection" was a knot he was still trying to unravel.

Given how interested the Kollective was in protecting this ship, surely that meant there was something alien about it?

Jamaal didn't know, but he was willing to spend a good deal of money to find out.

Fortunately, he had the credits to spare.

And Rosey was always looking to fluff up her own accounts.

Oh, Jamaal would still try to engage Rosey in the mystery, or the drama, but in the end, he knew it would be the credits that talked.

Not that he blamed her. It was nice to know your opponent's weaknesses.

As well as your friend's.

THREE

Princess Jun Ogawa searched the far eastern horizon once again, but there was no sign of the coming razor storm. The latest report she'd received from the starship she had in orbit around the planet Niani was that the storm wouldn't be there for another six hours, around the middle of the night. She still expected to see storm clouds on the horizon by now.

All she saw was a vast nothing. A few brave shrubs dotted the expansive flatlands, but those were seasonal and would be destroyed soon.

"Any change in storm predictions?" she asked out loud.

Though no other Human was on the surface with her, someone still replied.

"No change," came the smooth alto voice of Sano, her constant companion.

Sano was an AI housed in the pendant that Jun wore. It was about the size of a baby's fist, and looked like cheap costume jewelry, an amber thumbprint contained in a silver sphere. The pendant didn't contain all of the computer's processing—that was up on the ship in orbit. It did contain enough of Sano and her personality that Jun treated the sliver like the real AI.

In addition to her necklace, Jun wore an off-white, long-sleeved shirt, baggy black trousers, hard workman boots, and a gray hooded cloak. She wasn't covered due to some false sense of modesty—when not working, she generally wore skimpy shorts, sandals, and merely a vest for a top.

However, for the archaeological dig she'd been working on, covering up against the biting sand made much more sense. During the day, she also wore a large floppy hat and only changed over to the cloak at night, when the temperatures fell dramatically. She still carried her usual bag, containing a tablet with her notes and a bottle for water.

Sano continued. "Storm is still predicted to arrive around midnight local time. Are you sure you don't want to call your flitter now? Or just retreat to your starship?"

"I'm sure," Jun said. Someone had to wait for the cargo ship to pick up the last of the finds from the archaeological site. She'd been part of the team exploring the remains of one of the two known alien worlds, that of the Atoylee, a race that were frequently referred to as the sunflower people, given the appendages that looked like petals that grew around their faces.

All the dig's finds from the summer were packed up in a dozen large shipping containers, each roughly six feet cubed. She couldn't see over the tops of them, given her five feet tall height (not four foot eleven and a half inches, no matter what the damned measuring system said, thank you very much). The containers themselves were color-coded: the green ones contained actual artifacts, or at least what pieces and slivers remained after the cataclysm that had destroyed the planet. The two white containers held equipment, including onsite tablets, papers, and notes.

Or as her colleague once pointed out to her, the green unripe ones were those that needed additional time and research before maturing, along with the ripe white ones that were ready to pick and publish.

Jun personally felt as though the information contained in the white containers was less important. The archaeologists had found a treasure trove of actual papers detailing the work that the Atoylee had been doing in the lab the Humans had discovered. While the AIs had been able to do a rough translation, there were still too many gaps in their knowledge to figure out exactly what the alien papers said.

It was going to take time to discern the meaning of that writing. Time that the scientists hadn't had while at the dig.

Jun looked around and sighed. This dig had been her home for the last six months. She'd grown used to the wide-open space, the lack of greenery, the constant swishing of the wind across the white sand. She no longer minded the background smell of smoke and ash, or how it clogged her throat. At least Niani still had something of an atmosphere, and the air was breathable, if too warm out of the shade.

If Jun was being honest, without the threat of a razor storm, she might be tempted to stay planet side. The longer she stayed away from her starship, the longer before she had to answer the "important" summons from her family, telling her to return to the court. Again.

They didn't need her there. They just thought they did. She hadn't bothered to read the latest missive, assuming that it was some sort of manufactured crisis, as had been the previous ones.

Besides, Jun made much more of a difference down here. Sano—originally her governess, and now just minder and companion—was as fully trained a xenolinguist as Jun. Sano carried massive databases regarding all Human languages, everything they knew about the various Atoylee languages, as well as what had been found of the Harmaiz, the other alien race that Humans had discovered, who had also long since passed.

"I'll leave the surface before the storm hits," Jun promised Sano.

Razor storms were devastating, caused by hurricane-level winds hurling the planet's fine silicon grit with tremendous force. Because of the sharpness of the particles, they easily sliced through anything not protected, leaving it shredded, hence the name for these sorts of storms.

The storm season for Niani had been late that year, giving Jun and the other xenoarcheologists a few extra weeks at the dig site before buttoning everything down. She was expecting one last cargo ship that would pick up the few remaining shipping containers that needed to be hauled to safety.

It had better get there soon. The huge lights that they'd used to illuminate the dig had already been packed and hauled away. Working in the dark as the air grew thick and musty, winds kicking up dust everywhere, was not her idea of fun.

Then again, she had been the one to volunteer to stay behind with the last of the finds. No one at the site knew her true position, that she'd been one of the primary backers *funding* the dig.

Everyone there just thought of her as Jun Ogin, not as Princess Jun Ogawa. It wasn't as if she were in the direct line for the throne. Crown Princess Yumi was the official heir. Jun was merely a *hime*, a woman of noble birth. She did bear a faint resemblance to Yumi as well as the rest of the court, her hair black and fine and hanging like a curtain on those few occasions when she wore it down, her face flat with a slip of a nose peaking up, thin pinkish lips and dimples when she smiled. Her face was round like a moon, a term commonly used to describe someone thought of as pretty, not beautiful. Jun always thought her best feature were her eyes, dark and deep as a midnight pool.

Her father was the Empress Consort's cousin. It gave her the rank of princess, access to immense wealth, and once she'd reached twenty-one, six years before, the freedom to do her charitable work.

Which included following her passion, xenolinguistics.

Niani was the site of one of the two alien species that Humans had discovered so far in their explorations of the universe. Both had been destroyed by cataclysmic wars centuries before. Not the same war, despite circumstantial evidence to the contrary. They'd happened at different times, as far as the archaeologists were able to determine.

Both species had successfully bombed themselves out of existence, destroying their planets as a result.

At one time, Niani had been a thickly forested world. Now, it was covered in sand and soot. There were mountains in the far distant horizon, to the east, but for the most part, the land was flat, with slight undulating hills.

Part of the frustration with searching for Atoylee artifacts —the name a phonetic pronunciation of what the aliens had called themselves, at least as far as Jun and the others could determine—was that they'd been more biologically and chemically based than Humans. Their buildings had been organic, mostly grown, not built out of concrete.

The Atoylee had been bipedal, four-armed, vaguely Humanoid beings. A flare of petal-like appendages had surrounded their faces.

Everything surface level on Niani had been destroyed in the

LEAH R CUTTER

war, burned in fires that had raged planet wide. The Atoylee
hadn't built much underground, either.

Years before, a team had found a vault that had led to much
of Humanity's understanding of the Atoylee. That dig had
come upon a priceless find: a large collection of children's
books, including the equivalent of an ABC primer. Scientists
had been able to piece together much of the language using
those, at least simple terms.

It didn't help that the Atoylee language was made up of
multiple ancient writing systems that had been mashed
together. Their primary character set was composed of
logograms, like Chinese, with phonetic complements and
disambiguation symbols. It was read from the top to the
bottom of the page, and from right to left. However, their
writing also included something like Japanese katakana, for
spelling out foreign words—so pronunciation only, no clue as
to what the word actually meant.

This year, Jun and her team had found something equally
as important. The Atoylee had been a space-faring race. Early
teams had speculated that there might be some sort of habitat
on the closer of the two moons that circled Niani, but no one
had taken a closer look. No evidence supported the notion that
the Atoylee had found hyperspace. They had just been at the
start of their explorations.

However, mounting an archaeological dig on a moon with
little gravity and no atmosphere or water, hadn't been high on
anyone's list, particularly not when there was an entire planet
below with possible goodies to find.

Now, Jun wasn't sure that had been the wisest choice.
Particularly given what appeared to have been the scientific
laboratory that they'd found that year.

Yes, the lab they'd found had been dedicated to building

weapons. That was probably why it had been built underground in the first place.

The Atoylee hadn't been building explosive devices. Instead, this lab had been dedicated to some sort of chemical warfare.

According to the chemists the archaeologists had consulted, the weapons being developed wouldn't have destroyed the Atoylee. Not given their current understanding of the alien physiology.

In addition, the lab papers they'd found had also included hints that seemed to indicate that the Atoylee were either being attacked or were afraid of attack.

Jun couldn't wait to get back to the Institute of Xeno Studies (IXS) to spend more time pouring over the few documents they'd found, teasing out what nuances and secondary meanings she could find. See if she could figure out what exactly the Atoylee had been building in their lab, as well as who they'd been fighting.

More than one document had hinted at a second location for the chemical manufacturing.

Some people on the archaeological team had inisisted that it must have been located on Niani. Jun didn't think so. The papers had also mentioned Lawaka, which had been widely accepted as the name of the closer moon, though there was still some debate about that.

It was part of why Jun had agreed to stay behind. To guard those very important papers. Particularly since their scanner had broken two weeks before the end of the dig, so while most of the papers had been photographed, not everything had been scanned.

Plus, there was something special about working with the primary source material.

"Ship approaching," Sano said.

"Good," Jun said, turning toward the landing pad that had been set up outside of camp. Nothing much, just a paved area set apart from where the tents had been.

"Not good," Sano said. "I cannot identify the ship. It is also coming in hard and fast. Given its current course, it is not planning to land in the designated area."

"What?" Jun asked, confused. "Are they in trouble? Broadcasting a distress signal?"

"No," Sano said.

Jun hadn't heard such a disappointing tone in Sano's voice since the time Jun had refused a second date with the elder son of one of the royal families who hung around the court like parasites.

"They're pirates," Sano continued. "Hide."

FOUR

Dennis kept quiet while Rosey and Jamaal had their meeting.

Well. Mostly.

It wasn't as if they were trying to hide their conversation, or keep it private, or something. They were meeting in the kitchen area of *The Roadrunner*, after all. Jamal had brought some sort of fancy bread that Rosey had oohed and ahhed over, then they'd unsealed a pack of wine, and now they were seated and chatting in the breakfast nook that Dennis had *finally* perfected.

The dimensions had been the trickiest aspect of the space: making it big enough that the Humans didn't feel cramped while sitting in it, while at the same time, making it cozy.

Dennis had nearly despaired given the budget that Rosey had set for him. Couldn't she see how important this room was? She was going to be in there all the damned time! Of course it had to have a custom-built table. And benches. He could get off-the-shelf pillows and cushions, but really, it would have been so much better if he could have designed the fabric himself.

Still, those restraints had inspired him to greater levels of creativity, no matter what snide remarks some might make about an AI interior designer. Especially a frustrated one whose main job was to run the starship, not continually redesign it, as Rosey frequently reminded him.

She just didn't understand his art.

The table had been repurposed from a restaurant that had been going out of business. Solid golden wood laminate, rounded just so. The benches had also come second-hand and had barely required any touchup. They were a darker wood color than the table, and covered with cushions done in all various shades of red. The seats lifted up and revealed a large storage area for additional cushions and knick-knacks.

The walls in here were *not* holograms, no matter how much Dennis had begged and pleaded with Rosey. She said she didn't want them changing every day on his whim.

So Dennis had made do, with actual wallpaper (how quaint!) done in a painting of white brick. The bricks appeared to have the occasional bit broken off, revealing the red brick beneath, as well as a few strands of dark green ivy. The lamp over the table was particularly splendid, looking like a large, off-white globe. It gave off a golden light that could be dimmed or brightened as necessary.

All in all, Dennis was completely satisfied with his design. And true to his predictions, Rosey did spend a lot of time there, drinking her coffee in the morning and reading things on her tablet.

Of course, he would have added a hologram window on one side, with a sparkling fountain just past it, which would have given that essential sound element to a restful habitat, along with a bird feeder attracting various melodious birds. But Rosey had said no.

At least for now.

"So how did the Kollective end up with this ship, anyway?" Rosey asked Jamaal.

"I'm not exactly sure," Jamaal admitted.

"I know!" Dennis told them. "It seems that the Allied ship that found the wreck was a known pirate, and was picked up by a Kollective Defender during a border sweep."

At the slight pause that ensued, Dennis added, "I know what you're thinking. Those Defender ships are *such* an eyesore. Big, square, clunky things with no aesthetic sense."

"They're not meant to be pretty," Rosey said dryly. "Supposedly, they're intimidating."

Dennis gave the appropriate dismissive snort to such a concept. He could certainly outrun one if the need arose. Not something most people would know, though, given his original engine design.

While Dennis constantly tinkered with the interior of the ship, Rosey did the same to his engines, making quite a few modifications that gave *The Roadrunner* considerable speed in normal space, as well as quicker access to hyperspace than a regular starship.

He might even be able to outrun the obnoxious little stingerships that a Defender carried. A full complement was four dozen, supposedly flown by some of the best pilots out there.

He had his doubts, especially given the pilots he'd met and had seen Rosey race against.

The stingerships were small fighters, just big enough to carry pilots and laser cannons. The rear of each ship rose up behind it, then faced forward over the pilot's head, like a scorpion's tail. It fired what was colloquially called a disintegration beam.

The beam "ate" metal, porcelain, and rubber. Basically, every material used to make up a ship. It would start as a small hole then spread. While Dennis understood the physics of it, he also agreed with the common term used for it.

Not that he had nightmares about one of those beams being used on *The Roadrunner*.

A stingership could only fire the disintegration beam once. Then, it was done for, and the pilot would need to be rescued. (Which seemed like such a bad, *wasteful* design to Dennis. Then again, it was the Kollective.) In addition, the disintegration beam wasn't clean, and sometimes the stingership firing the beam would also be eaten after the beam had been fired.

Seemed that if the pilot had any implants, such as the common enough bone phone, they, too, would be eaten.

"So where exactly is this supposed alien ship?" Rosey asked.

"It's actually been landed on a planet," Jamaal said. He sounded as disgusted by the fact as Dennis was. "The planet's name is New Arrakis, if you can believe that. Historic literary reference," Jamaal continued when Rosey looked puzzled.

Dennis had to look up the reference.

"What, a desert planet?" he complained.

"Don't worry, sweetheart, I'll take a flitter down to the surface," Rosey assured him.

"That won't be any better and you know it," Dennis complained. "All that dust and sand that you'll carry with you! I'll never get the carpets clean again. I'll just have to replace them all."

Rosey sighed. "If you don't mind? We need to finish our negotiations here."

"Fine," Dennis said as he called up a catalog with the latest carpet designs and tried not to listen.

There really wasn't anywhere on the starship that he couldn't hear, though he did respect Rosey's privacy and didn't listen in when she was in her bathroom or her bedroom. Particularly not when she was entertaining guests. They did have an agreement, though, that if she ever called his name, he could listen in.

And while technically she hadn't called him, they *were* discussing a supposed alien starship.

Though Rosey had a lot of experience with ships, she wasn't actually a ship.

Not like Dennis.

While Rosey bargained hard, Dennis still felt as though Jamaal got the better end of the deal. *He* wasn't the one who was going to have to deal with all that grit clogging his air filters.

After Jamaal had left, Dennis may have complained a little—just a little—to Rosey about this new job they'd taken.

At least until she promised him that half the finder's fee would go to his decorating fund.

"Words to make my heart sing!" Dennis said, happily settling down.

Maybe he could finally get some workers in to move that one wall in the business conference room. The room was at least a full foot too short, and really ruined the *feng shui* of that entire region of the ship.

Rosey did a quick pass through the living areas of the ship, ensuring that everything was strapped down. Not that they'd necessarily lose gravity while in hyperspace. However, strange things did happen there occasionally.

The jump they were making wasn't that far. Rosey went through the official preflight checklist. She was a stickler for those sorts of things, even though Dennis could go through the list in a quarter of the time.

However, it was better for Rosey's state of mind to be precise and planned. No matter how much or how often she went by instinct when racing.

Finally, Dennis was able to release himself from where he was tethered to *Lorenzo* and headed out to the jump area.

He wasn't anticipating that Rosey would find an actual alien starship. Instead, he stayed focused on the new carpets he might buy.

And the new air filters as well.

FIVE

Moe hated the saying, "If it weren't for bad luck, I'd have no luck at all."

Particularly since it appeared to be true, at least at this time in his life, as he sat alone in the main helm of the starship *Aisha*, piloting the ship toward their destination, the planet Niani.

Everything around him was worn or second-hand. The cushions of the pilot's chair were held together with straps, which left bruises across his back if he wasn't careful when accelerating and decelerating. Half the controls on the panel before him weren't lit, and he didn't trust the half that were. A slightly burnt scent stayed in the air, no matter how many times he replaced the air filters. The temperature was at least constant, and a bit warmer than other ships, on purpose, because Moe liked being able to walk around in a light T-shirt, shorts, and sandals.

Only the engines were worth anything at all, and that was in part due to Atilio, his mechanic and long-term buddy, who hadn't abandoned Moe, even now, during the worst time of his life.

Moe had supposedly been born lucky. He was seventh son of a seventh son. His parents had even given him seven names, to commemorate such a rare occurrence: Mohammed Abdul Nuwan Pradeep Aruna Tennakoon Herath.

Most people just called him Moe these days. He'd been told he didn't look like a Moe, with his straight black hair, proud hooked nose, brown eyes and thin lips. His skin always looked darkly tanned compared to the Anglos he dealt with. He wasn't sure what a Moe looked like, except for what he saw in the mirror.

He wasn't ashamed of his family, or even his name—he genuinely felt sorry for those people who only had two names, three at best. They had no wealth of family or history.

At the same time, he rarely went back to his home planet of Ghaybi.

When he'd first set out hauling cargo, ten years before when he'd just turned eighteen, he'd been certain that he was going to make it big. Such plans, such schemes he'd had!

It hadn't taken him long to buy *Aisha*, to start making longer cargo runs. Of course, the bank still held the majority of her, and he had another balloon payment due soon.

That was one of the things that he made damned sure kept running on the ship: the merchant's clock, which gave an accurate representation of time as it was kept on the bank's planet. No matter where else he traveled, that constant ticking always plagued him, even following him into his dreams (or more likely, nightmares). The bank had installed it when he'd taken out the loan on his ship.

He was not going to lose *Aisha*, not on top of everything else.

The stars he could see out of the front viewport looked like all the other stars he'd seen before, beautiful and distant. He told himself that this was just a regular run, like all the runs he'd made over the years.

A deep pit of guilt and despair roiling in the center of his stomach told otherwise.

There was a famous poem that Moe half-remembered from his time in school. Every stanza ended with the phrase, "That is, not to go home in X," where the last word was changed every time.

At first, the young man makes his fortune and doesn't go home in success.

Then, the young man loses his fortune, and so doesn't go home in despair.

Eventually, the young man is killed, and so doesn't go home in death.

Moe hoped that he would find success again, that he wasn't going to die and not go home again, his parents never learning his true fate.

Which was where he was sure to end up if this trip didn't go well.

Moe had made a bargain with the devil, that was certain. Constantine was the biggest warlord in the sector of Allied Worlds' space where Moe had run into trouble.

Constantine could be charming. And he had the money and influence that Moe lacked. While they might have the same number of contacts, friends and acquaintances they could call on, Moe's were more-or-less legitimate.

Whereas Constantine's were definitely on the other side of the law.

However, it was either deal with the warlord Constantine, do a series of jobs for him so Moe could dig his way out of debt, or sell *Aisha* and try to make a living on a planet somewhere.

And never truly see the stars again.

"What's that smell, boss?" Atilio asked as he came into the helm, sitting in the co-pilot's chair and strapping himself in.

It wasn't as if Atilio could fly. Sure, he could handle the controls if the ship was on autopilot. That was about it.

However, he did come and sit in the other seat regularly to keep Moe company now and again, as there was no longer a co-pilot. Or a purser, keeping track of their cargo. Or any of the dozen or so crew that should be on a starship like *Aisha*.

Instead, it was Moe, Atilio, and Constantine's three goons.

Moe sniffed the air in the helm. He couldn't smell anything other than the usual; the dust from surfaces that all needed cleaning, singed wiring that they'd recently fixed, and maybe a hint of the protein packs that the goons ate.

"I don't smell anything," he said, already starting to worry. Was there something else going wrong on the ship?

"I don't know. Smells like the brood is getting thick up in here," Atilio said with a cheeky grin.

Moe opened him mouth then closed it again, choosing to merely glare at Atilio.

They were opposites in many ways. Atilio had reddish-brown curly hair, hazel eyes, and skin that was lighter than Moe's. Not white enough to be called an Anglo, but still on the lighter side of things. While Moe was tall and lean, six foot three and all leg, Atilio was only five foot nine, stocky and muscular. Moe also tended to be more serious, and Atilio was always the one with a smile or a joke. Atilio was older, not quite twice Moe's age, but close.

And Moe hadn't been brooding. Really.

Okay, so maybe he'd been brooding a bit.

With the way his life had been going recently, he deserved a good brood now and again.

"This job has to go well," Moe said quietly. He didn't think the three goons could hear him. The last he'd checked, they were all eating (again!) in the kitchen.

On one side of the kitchen were storage containers and heating elements for putting together quick meals. He couldn't afford an aeroponics system, let alone a hydroponics system, or even a food printer. He carried cans and packets of pre-made meals, then stocked up at nearly every port he called on. As he never made a run more than a week or two, it didn't make sense to carry anything more.

The other side of the kitchen held a large table, big enough for sixteen to easily fit around it, the full complement of crew and then some. Moe had tried to take the table apart, but it was bolted together, as well as welded to the floor, and was more bother than it was worth.

He left it there as a reminder of happier times, when he'd had more people on the ship. And of times to come, when he could afford more again.

Even if it made the room echo and made Moe feel depressed, with all those empty seats.

"The job will go fine," Atilio assured him. "And if it doesn't, we'll find something else," he added with a shrug.

"There isn't anything else," Moe said. He couldn't get a legitimate cargo without a crew to help him care for it. And he couldn't get a crew until he had some money to pay them.

"We're still alive, aren't we?" Atilio pointed out. "And as long as that doesn't change, we still have a chance. Your luck will come back."

Moe pressed his lips together, unwilling to say anything.

He did still have his luck.

It had just all been bad.

Which was why he was about to go and steal some alien artifacts from an undefended, empty archaeological dig.

His family was never going to understand.

Maybe someday he'd figure out how to not go back home in shame.

SIX

Rosey didn't like being in hyperspace. She didn't know anyone who did.

It was convenient. It allowed Humanity to travel at faster than light speeds.

It was also off-putting.

In hyperspace, the lights in the main helm of *The Road-runner* held a reddish hue that no adjusting of spectrums could counterbalance. Many of them bore slight halos. Every straight surface appeared to be outlined in thick black, giving the controls in front of her a cartoony look. The air had a bitter tang to it, like someone had burned rubber wiring. It also felt warmer in hyperspace, no matter what the temperature reading on her console said.

The most accurate description Rosey had heard of how being in hyperspace felt was that she'd taken a step to the side and was now viewing everything at a strange angle.

Fortunately, the run to New Arrakis wouldn't take that long to make. Four hours in real time, though subjectively it might feel like a couple of days.

No danger of getting shredded, not in this short of a run, particularly with the new improved shielding that Rosey had installed on *The Roadrunner.*

Rosey didn't understand all the physics of the phenomenon of shredding. She suspected that there were only a few mega-brained scientists who did.

When Humanity had discovered hyperspace, of course they'd sent unmanned drones through at the start, just to make sure it was safe.

The first manned trip was just a little longer than one made by the drones.

It made all the difference in terms of side effects.

Rosey had morbidly watched more than one recording of what happened when a drone ship without adequate shielding went through hyperspace.

Everything was normal at the beginning—just the normal weird lighting and heavy lines that always occurred in hyperspace. Once the starship (or drone) had been in space a specific amount of time, there was a jolt, as if the ship had just passed through a strong barrier. Then the shaking began, a slight trembling of the camera that never got any worse or any better.

A brief time after the shaking started, lines appeared on the walls, like fractures, though strangely parallel, not spidering out. They weren't deep cuts, just black marks, as if parts of the physical plane have been replaced with nothingness.

Then, between one breath and the next, the place was shredded. It was as if a large-clawed monster has winked into existence, raked its claws down every surface, carving ribbons out of the walls, the furniture, everything. Then the creature vanished again.

If the ship made it back to realtime quickly enough at that

point, the exterior was spared from such treatment. If not, the entire ship would eventually be shredded.

The first manned ship through hyperspace had been shredded, the Human occupants lost, their bodies torn to pieces.

It took time for the scientists to develop the shielding that was now standard on every starship. And they kept pushing the envelope, creating better shielding that was lightweight enough to not put a strain on the engines while at the same time, protecting the precious cargo inside. Better shields allowed starships to be in hyperspace for longer and longer periods of time. The last Rosey heard, they'd pushed the time out to fourteen hours.

Rosey made sure to regularly update *The Roadrunner* with the best, most stable shields she could afford, once every five to eight years. She didn't bother with the most experimental. No, let some other fool gamble on those. She waited until the technology had been tested by people other than her, so a few years after the latest batch had been developed. *The Roadrunner* could survive being in hyperspace for at least ten hours, going all the way from the innermost planets of the Kollective to the start of the Allied Worlds' territory.

Maybe she could get eleven out of what she had, but she wouldn't push it.

Dennis didn't need to announce their arrival into real time. Rosey felt it when they popped back up, an unrealized pressure releasing her chest, the lights suddenly normal and the surfaces clean again.

"So where we at?" Rosey asked as the console in front of her lit up.

"About three hours out from the planet," Dennis said.

Normally, those sorts of estimations would come from a copilot. However, Rosey preferred to travel by herself. It was one of the reasons why she had Dennis, and had automated as much of the flying of the starship as she felt comfortable with.

The Roadrunner could never land on a planet. It was over a hundred yards long. Someone had once told her that it was about the size of an American football field, a reference she'd had to look up. Most of the space on the starship was taken up with engines and cargo holds. Rosey had the holds configured so she could deliver up to four speedships at a time.

While Dennis might have her permission to redesign the living areas of the starship, she wouldn't allow him to do much to the cargo holds, in part because she didn't want him spending money there. Those needed to be functional, not pretty.

Dennis didn't always understand that distinction.

When Rosey had asked for a personality module attached to the AI, she hadn't anticipated that Dennis would "grow up" as it were, and decide that he actually wanted to be an interior designer. She'd heard of other, stranger personalities that AIs had developed as they matured. Like the poor captain whose AI was a frustrated sommelier, unable to actually taste any of the wines she procured.

At least Dennis could "see" his handiwork. Rosey had learned early on to give Dennis his own budget for decorating, and to never question too closely where the money went.

It made Dennis happy, and while she might occasionally complain about the changes, it was nice to not always be living in the same colors and rooms.

Even if he did sometimes take it a little too far...

Rosey set a course for New Arrakis (really, couldn't they have come up with a better name?) and went back to her rooms to spend a few moments in a sonic cleansing unit. Going through hyperspace always left her feeling dirty. And a little nauseated, so she ate the last of the fantastic focaccia that Jamaal had brought to sweeten their deal.

Finally, the ship arrived at the planet. It looked like a red marble hanging there, though even from space she could see touches of green close to both the poles, while all along the equator was reddish-gold desert.

Supposedly, no one lived in the hottest places, though Rosey wouldn't take that bet. People were strange, and occasionally desperate, and those sorts of people would make decisions no one sane would.

Which included some fairly illegal or at least morally questionable genetic engineering to be able to survive such an environment.

The Kollective frowned on almost all genetic manipulation, except to save the life of the child. The Empire was more forward thinking, and gene cleaning was an accepted, standard practice, to help their citizens be healthy and not encumbered by diseases that could easily be cured by just a few tweaks.

Most of the serious genetic engineering occurred out in the Allied Worlds. People with mushroom-shaped heads where they stuffed in more brains. Others who were preternaturally beautiful, every feature perfectly symmetrical. Still others who were as much machine as meat, powerful cyborg bullies who acted as warlords.

That was where the design team of J4 had come from. They were four male clones who worked together to create outlandish starships.

J4 models were one of a kind, designed to fit the client's specifications. Rosey thought some of ships they'd made were truly ugly, but they probably had made the client happy. Like the starship that was a solid cube of metal, some historic cultural reference she didn't get.

One of the things that all J4 ships had in common were the lights. They'd started off their career building ships for a client they called "Captain Lensflare." The design element had stuck, and so they had lights that slanted just so on every single ship they created.

The last two spaceships that Jamaal had paid for Rosey to visit had turned out to be J4 ships. Some asshole with more money than sense had paid for them to be built, then abandoned them out on the edges of space. Possibly the same jerk. Twice.

The second one, Rosey had only had to glance at it to know that it wasn't alien.

The lights always gave it away.

While Rosey didn't gamble, she was still willing to bet that the ship on the planet below was just another J4 design.

She'd find out soon enough.

SEVEN

Jun had no idea where to hide. There were twelve shipping containers scattered over the flat ground, where there used to be equipment tents and sleeping accommodations. The tunnel leading to the underground area they'd discovered was well secured against the coming storm season. There were no handy trees, bushes, or rocks for her to duck behind.

All she had was her cloak. Maybe she could go squat down outside of what was clearly the camp area, and pretend to be a boulder?

Unable to think of anything else, Jun hurried to the side of the dig and squatted down. Luckily, due to all the work she'd done that summer on the dig, her leg muscles didn't protest too much. She'd spent far too many hours in this exact position, patiently brushing away the accumulated sand and dust from precious artifacts.

Jun pulled her cloak around her, then breathed deeply, growing very still. She didn't allow her thoughts to stick. Instead, she let them flow, one after another, not attaching anything of significance to them.

The ship landed. It wasn't a proper spaceship, able to travel between planets in a system, but just a type of flitter, that went from a ship, down onto a planet, then back up again. It looked old and pieced together out of spare parts.

Probably from the Allied Worlds, but Jun didn't allow any anger at that thought. It came and went with her slow breathing.

A large ramp rolled out from the rear end of the ship. A tall man with dark brown skin and straight black hair scanned the area with binoculars, but he didn't see her. Maybe he wasn't looking for heat signatures.

Behind him, three pirates walked out, down the ramp, with powered dollies for picking up the shipping containers. Of course, they went for the green ones first, the ones primarily containing artifacts.

Jun barely contained her growl, though she doubted anyone would be able to hear it. The wind was picking up. She submerged it with yet another deep breath, letting the emotion flow out of her.

Had someone on the dig told the pirates about their finds? Or was it merely luck that they initially hauled those away?

The planets of Niani and Zonami, where the alien Huzzomi had once lived, were considered part of intergalactic space. No single government controlled them, even though Niani was in territory that would normally be part of the Empire, and Zonami was in Allied space. All alien artifacts went to museums and universities for study and research. No one was supposed to be able to own or collect alien artifacts. It was illegal, though the penalties did vary across systems.

However, Jun knew exactly the type of people who robbed archaeological digs. Or rather, who would pay for such a theft. Not someone from her direct family, no. The Empire did have severe penalties if they caught such a collector. But some of the hangers-on at the court might consider it a point of pride to have a private collection of alien goods.

This ship was probably from the Allied Worlds, as there were dozens of rich men and women who would fund this piracy.

There appeared to be five pirates total. Three who were doing all the work, manning the dollies, and two who stood back near the wide-open door of the ship, obviously keeping watch.

Jun didn't believe in any of the gods that her family was required to ritualistically sacrifice to, but just then, she sent a prayer to the Goddess of Scholars, asking that the pirates leave behind the white containers. The ones that held the papers that had yet to be properly scanned.

No such luck.

After the green containers were all loaded, there seemed to be a quick debate about the remaining four white ones.

Jun studied the group. Though for her, people were harder to read than ancient Japanese texts, she'd still bet that the three doing the work were the ones who wanted to pick up the white boxes, while the two keeping watch would have left them.

The three workers won.

At least the two keeping watch left their posts after that.

All the pirates were inside the ship for a few minutes as they stored the first of the white containers on the ship.

A sharp tug of wind fluttered Jun's cloak.

Jun risked checking over her shoulder.

The storm clouds she'd been expecting now massed all the way across the horizon. The air grew thick with dust alarmingly fast, practically between one breath and the next.

When Jun looked back at the flitter, she realized just how

hazy the air had gotten. She could only see the little ship due to the light pouring out of the open ramp.

She had to stop these pirates from stealing all her hard work. Once they disappeared into Allied space, she'd never be able to track them down, not even with all of her considerable wealth and influence.

And the person or persons who'd funded this theft would be adept at keeping their "collection" private.

Jun growled, this time out loud.

"You aren't about to do something foolish, are you?" Sano murmured.

While Jun didn't have a bonephone, or any improvements of that nature, she did have an earpiece that she wore deep in her ear cannel. Only a doctor's examination would discover it. The only one who could access it was Sano.

"Tell the family that I've been delayed. Got it?" Jun said. Though the wind tore the whispered words out of her mouth as she spoke them, she had no doubt that Sano heard.

"It's my job to protect you," Sano said.

"It's also your job to obey me," Jun reminded the AI.

Before she'd turned eighteen, Sano had been Jun's governess and able to ignore her charge's direct commands. The day after her birthday, Jun went to have Sano reprogrammed to follow her instructions.

When her parents had protested, Jun had reminded them that she no longer was required to wear Sano at all. Their choice was either to allow her to reprogram the AI, or for Jun to never wear one again. If there was ever any trouble, for example, if she was kidnapped, she couldn't be located using the AI.

Jun had never been the stubborn one in her family. That designation had gone to her eldest brother Daiki, who'd refused to be a proper first-born pretty much from day one.

Luckily, her middle brother Minato was easy going, happy to follow along and be in the court, while her eldest brother lived as a hermit blowing glass on the grand coast. She was the youngest and so was allowed to go her own way most of the time (and she was not as spoiled as her two brothers often teased her).

That didn't mean that Jun couldn't put her foot down when need arose.

"Don't go stowaway on that ship," Sano said.

"I have to know where the containers are being taken," Jun replied. She darted forward, the winds pushing her to the side as she neared the wide-open mouth of the flitter. She managed to duck down to the side of the ramp as the three pirates made their last trip to the surface.

Jun was thankful once again for all the work she'd done that summer on the dig. It was fairly easy for her to pull herself up, onto the ramp, then scurry inside.

She only had a few moments to look around and make her way to the cargo bay. The other containers had already been tied down, black straps securing them against the sides of the hold.

Her gray cloak would help hide her in the cargo area, as it was close to the color of the scarred and dented metal that made up the interior of this area of the ship.

Jun slipped between two of the containers, turning her back to the opening, then squatted down again.

After the flitter took off, Jun would be able to find a better hiding space. Where she was would have to do for now.

She calmed her breathing and her rapidly beating heart as the last shipping container was loaded and strapped in. A short while after that, a vibration started under her feet, shaking the sides of the ship.

"What are you going to do when they find you?" Sano asked.

Amazing how dry the AI managed to sound, even over the thrumming of the engines.

"Play the princess card," Jun said after a moment. The sorts of people who would steal alien artifacts would also ransom her in a heartbeat.

"Do I even have to point out the numerous ways that could go wrong?" Sano said.

"No," Jun said. She tried not to grin. She told herself she should be scared. This was not some grand adventure she was about to embark on. She was locked in a ship with desperate men engaged in desperate deeds.

She was an academic. Not some adventurer.

The thrumming of the ship under her feet said otherwise, and she wasn't going to protest too loudly.

At least not yet.

EIGHT

Duri Chung sat cursing in her small office. She was quiet about it, though, so that not even the listening device under her desk would hear. (She hated calling them bugs. That made it feel as though the room was *unclean*, as opposed to it being just an SOP.)

As a Director in the Kollective, one of the highest levels of civil service attainable, Duri didn't bother removing the listening devices from her office. Instead, she took pride in the fact that someone considered her enough of a threat to listen in on her conversations. Whoever had placed the device had put it under her plain wooden desk, which meant they understood where the power in her office lay: directly with her and not with those who visited, sitting in one of the three comfortable chairs on the other side.

There wasn't much more to the office beyond those furnishings: a small credenza securing her less-than-important papers; a coatrack next to the door holding many coats and scarves, due to the changeable weather on the planet of New

Rome; a mini-fridge that frequently had to be cleaned out due to the lunches she forget to eat, with a collection of the expected photographs of her family and important events in her life displayed on top of it.

Duri knew her place in the byzantine hierarchy that made up the Kollective bureaucracy. She was actually higher than her title indicated, with easy access to generals and admirals, as well as some of the lead scientists. Lower than she'd like, as the Grand Assembly didn't regularly call on her to give her reports in person.

For now.

That was all going to change with the alien ship that had been discovered.

In the meantime, the idiot captain of the Defender who'd found the alien ship in the first place was heading for a world of hurt.

It was a standing order that any ship of unknown origin was to be *immediately* reported to her office. Particularly if it looked alien in the slightest. It didn't matter if it turned out to be another of those obnoxious J4 fakes. She still needed to be informed.

And *immediately* meant as soon as the Defender reached a station capable of transmitting news back to the Kollective. Not whenever they finally got around to it, or felt like it, or any number of lame excuses that Duri had heard over the years.

Fortunately, Captain "I'm Too Important To Report The Alien Ship In My Hold" was about to have a life lesson in obeying orders.

Particularly orders from her office.

She wouldn't ask for his demotion. Not unless the ship actually did turn out to be of alien manufacture.

However, she would insist that a black mark be placed permanently in his record. One that no amount of doing good in other sectors would ever erase.

Eventually, the idiotic captain would figure out that he was never getting promoted.

Ever again.

He'd have to become some goddamned war hero for that mark to be expunged.

And there just weren't any good wars brewing on the horizon. Humanity was at a surprisingly peaceful lull in their history. Having enough planets for people to immigrate to had done wonders for that infamous Human aggression, primarily by relieving the pressures of living on a single world.

It also helped to have planets that government could use to ship people off to when they couldn't be rehabilitated.

Let some other government handle the miscreants, like the Allied Worlds—which honestly, was barely a government, even in name.

Duri calmed herself with a few deep breaths, then ordered fresh hot green tea from her latest assistant while she browsed through a few meaningless reports on her tablet, biding her time. She knew that she presented as completely calm, even serene, having perfected the "inscrutable Asian look" when she'd been a child, lying to her parents about where she'd found so many credits, never telling them of the protection racket she'd set up in the neighborhood. She wore her black hair collar length, with cute bangs to slightly ameliorate the fierceness of her scowl. Her large dark eyes always held a hint of menace, or at least she'd been told that. (She still considered it one of the highest compliments she'd ever received.) She wore an office casual outfit as she wasn't expecting to see anyone important that day, just an off-white blouse and peach colored skirt. She had a flashier dress hanging on the coatrack, beautiful but severe, that could either be dressed up to be distracting, or dressed down to merely appear Important.

Eventually, her assistant arrived with the tea, then left. She'd been quick and unobtrusive, but she hadn't been working for the department long enough for Duri to bother remembering her name.

After disciplining herself to take a sip of the perfectly made tea did Duri bring back up the report she had. Of course, it had initially come in electronically, through a regular channel. There was no Top Secret classification on it. The stupid captain hadn't even secured the transmission.

Fool.

All that meant was that there were probably bounty hunters already on the way to the ship's location. She wasn't naïve enough to believe that the military facility where the alien ship was currently being kept would hold them at bay. Not in a place as backwards as New Arrakis.

She'd chase them off quickly enough. And she was fairly certain that they wouldn't have the means to steal the ship.

No, it was in *her* possession now.

The proof that there were live aliens out there. It was her job to make sure that it was the Kollective about to make first contact with them.

When Duri had been a child, she'd had childish dreams about meeting one of the Atoylee sunflower people. But cold hard physics set in: time travel didn't work, and scientists had too many moral and ethical quandaries about possibly bringing one of the aliens back via cloning. (Though she'd change that, too, when—not if—she got powerful enough.)

So Duri had shifted her passion to finding the other aliens

who were sure to be out there. Because she was smart, made good connections, and was ruthless in her approach, she'd carved herself a space in the Kollective government bureaucracy, getting them to pay for her obsession, becoming the Director of the office for the Search for Live Contact (SLC). She had only a single assistant, but that didn't matter.

All the naysayers in her family, like her great-aunt, would have to eat their words one day. She'd make sure of it.

Duri had destroyed all of the electronic copies of the report that existed out on the Kollective computer systems. Too late, but it was at least the start of the security measures she would need to take. The only electronic copy that remained was on her air gapped tablet, the one that didn't even have the ability to connect to the Net, the intergalactic collection of electronic servers that held all of the wisdom, as well as all of the foolishness, of Humanity.

Now, she pored over printed copies, looking at the electronic versions now and again, sizing and resizing the picture, drilling in to look at details then out again to try to get a glimpse of the entire craft.

The stupid purser who'd finally reported the alien ship had done a haphazard job of a preliminary scan. Really, the only thing that had raised any flags that the craft might be alien was that the metal composition was so very different than anything Human made.

Was it alien? The resolution just wasn't good enough for her to be able to tell, not one hundred percent.

Fortunately, Duri had also learned patience at a young age. She'd already sent out a military retrieval team to bring the ship to her. They, at least, understood the need for secrecy, and so additional information about the ship wasn't about to leak out.

In the meanwhile, there were other reports to review. Budgets to be calculated. Other supposed alien sightings to be investigated.

Her prize for all her patient work would arrive soon.

She was certain of it.

NINE

Jamaal did not curse when he discovered that all the official reports of the alien wreck had been eliminated. He had copies, of course. As did other hunters, he was certain.

However, the disappearing reports meant that Duri Chung, the Director of the SLC, was now involved.

Jamaal sat back in his computer chair, his eyes narrowed at his screen, as he considered his options.

Since he was no longer employed by the Emperor, he didn't have the resources he once did. He couldn't call on a shadowy intelligence agency to get the most recent reports on Duri and her movements. He couldn't send some young operative into the field to keep watch over her.

It didn't matter that he couldn't order a hack on her computer systems, to find all that he could. He knew that that the only remaining electronic copies of the report of the alien wreck were on that damned air-gapped tablet. That was Duri's SOP.

She'd probably sent an expert team to extract the ship from its current location, people who actually knew what they were doing, as opposed to the skeleton crew of misfits guarding it on New Arrakis.

Jamaal sent a message to Rosey via Dennis to warn her of the coming crew. The credentials he'd drawn up for her would get her into the military base on New Arrakis without problems. They didn't have the resources to dig deep enough to find holes in her cover story.

The other team, though—if they questioned her, or examined her papers closely...

It worried Jamaal. Particularly since it would be a while before his message arrived.

The message Jamaal had sent wouldn't be transmitted directly. Humanity had never invented something like an ansible, and could not instantly communicate across the huge swaths of space. Instead, they had the equivalent of the pony express: ships that made regular runs carrying messages between worlds and space stations.

If the Kollective incarcerated Rosey, well, Jamaal still had a few strings he could pull.

He could also break her out if absolutely necessary.

In the meantime, what was he going to do about Duri?

He didn't want to kill her. Not yet. Removing her would just create a vacuum, and someone else would step in to fill that position.

Jamaal would just as soon deal with the devil he knew rather than roll the dice and hope that someone less capable might step up.

Could he get the ship away from Duri? With minimal bloodshed? Particularly if they didn't have Rosey?

Just how badly did he want to keep proof of aliens away from Duri and the Kollective?

How much of a crime would it be to destroy it? Along

with all evidence that it had ever existed? Just to keep it out of the Kollective's hands?

"I know that look," came a deep voice from behind Jamaal.

Jamaal blinked and shook his head, coming back from the dark places his soul had dipped into. He pasted on a smile and turned to look at Harkeen.

Harkeen's skin was as black as his name indicated. It practically glowed in bright light. Today, he wore a bright red short-sleeved shirt that seemed to highlight that ebony, with tan shorts. Like Jamaal, Harkeen wore his hair buzzed short, though he had a stylish design of lightning bolts carved into the sides. They were of equal height, just a shade over six feet tall. While Jamaal was thin and angular, Harkeen was wider and thicker everywhere.

Harkeen took one look at Jamaal, sighed and shook his head, crossing his arms over his broad chest.

"What?" Jamaal asked, aiming for an innocent tone.

From the look Harkeen shot him, he'd missed by a good distance.

"You're thinking about eliminating the competition," Harkeen said. He held up his hand before Jamaal could explain. "Is it necessary?"

Jamaal took a deep breath and sat back in his chair.

How important was it to keep this alien wreck out of the hands of the Kollective?

If this ship led to scientific advances, the Kollective wouldn't share them.

It would be awful if the Kollective had live contact with the aliens first. It would be the worst first impression that Humanity could possibly make. Even Allied Worlds representatives would be better.

"I believe it's starting to become necessary," Jamaal said slowly.

Harkeen nodded. "I trust you, and your judgment," he said softly.

A hard knot that Jamaal hadn't even realized had gathered in the center of his chest, weighing him down, lifted so suddenly he felt dizzy.

"Thank you," he said, holding out his hand.

Harkeen took it in his beefy one.

As Jamaal suspected, his entire body had grown cold when he'd slipped into that other persona, away from Jamaal the genial, gregarious merchant, and back into Jamaal the assassin.

"How dangerous is it going to be?" Harkeen asked, bringing Jamaal's hand up to his chest so that Jamaal could feel the steady heartbeat under the solid muscles.

"Not very," Jamaal said. When Harkeen gave him that *look*, he added hastily, "No, really. It isn't a high official with serious security, and they'll still be breathing afterward."

Probably. Killing Duri was always going to be an option, though at this point, it really was the last resort.

"I trust you to make the right call," Harkeen said. "And, more importantly, to always come back to me."

Jamaal peered more closely at Harkeen. Before Jamaal had retired, they'd had an open relationship, coming and going as they'd pleased. It had only been since Jamaal had retired that they'd been a lot more "on" than "off."

However, his lover didn't appear to be asking for the sort of commitment that Jamaal couldn't make. Not really. Not yet, at any rate.

Possibly not ever, though he didn't know that for certain.

"I'll always come back to you, babe," Jamaal said, smoothly

rising so he could draw closer to Harkeen, bask in the warmth and strength of the other man.

Harkeen merely rolled his eyes at Jamaal. "Just see that you do." He gave Jamaal a hard peck, not the extended kiss that Jamaal had been angling for.

Then Harkeen stepped back. "When do you leave?"

Jamaal sighed and also took a step back. "Now," he said, glancing around the room. He always had a "go" bag packed and ready, just in case. It contained outfits for all occasions, as well as weapons.

Harkeen nodded, stepping forward and dragging Jamaal to him, giving him the extended kiss full of passion that Jamaal had been hoping for.

After a timeless time, Harkeen loosened his hold on Jamaal.

Jamaal held on, squeezing the big man one last time, before he let go.

"I will come back to you," he promised.

"Just see that you do," Harkeen said, turning and walking out of the room.

Jamaal took a deep breath, feeling centered even as the outer layers peeled away.

He had a mission. Two, actually, though he'd just send people to take care of the ship, while he personally dealt with Duri.

Time to get moving.

TEN

Moe was glad to be back on *Aisha* again, particularly after the quick trip down to the planet.

Everything had gone as planned. The archaeological site had been empty, even though the first time he'd scanned the area from the flitter, he'd found a suspicious heat signature.

However, as it had disappeared by the time he got back to the controls of the ship, he assumed it had just been a false reading. The little skiff was old and needed as many repairs as *Aisha* did. On the planet, he didn't have fancy binoculars that let him see in the infra-red, just plain optics. He hadn't spotted anything with those either.

The three goons had loaded up the cargo hold quickly enough, though Atilio had complained about how loosely some of the storage cubes had been strapped down after the flitter had pulled into *Aisha*.

Now, they were on their way back to the Allied Worlds, back to Constantine, on the planet Psykee.

It was some sort of mythological reference that Moe had never bothered to look up.

Because *Aisha* was an older ship, she didn't have the best shielding. This meant that instead of taking two or three long trips through hyperspace to get to their destination, they had to make over a dozen skips.

And in between every jump, Atilio had to recalibrate the engines, the shields, or whatever else had shaken loose. This required them to be in space a lot longer, five days there and just as many back.

Fortunately, they'd been prepared for this long of a trip at the start, and had packed enough supplies for two weeks so they didn't have to stop someplace and resupply.

They'd just come out of hyperspace in Allied World's territory. If Atilio could get the engines to cooperate, they'd be back at Psykee in two days. Otherwise, it might take three.

"Captain, can you come down to the engine room?" Atilio's voice suddenly sounded on the intercom.

Worried, Moe rose from the pilot's chair and hurried to the back of the ship.

The engine room was actually below the deck, while engineering, itself was on the same level. Moe glanced quickly at the dials above the main control station, but just because everything appeared to be green and glowing didn't mean there wasn't something horribly wrong. He didn't smell anything burning, though it did seem as though the engines were running louder than normal.

Light shone out of a hole in the floor at the far end of engineering. Moe hurried over and squatted down, spotting Atilio just under the hatch. He stood with what looked like a regular wrench in his hand, loosening the bolts on a panel in order to get at the guts. The walls of the small space were lined with equipment, tubes, and bundles of wire.

"What's up?" Moe asked. He didn't bother climbing

down the ladder after Atilio. There was barely enough room for one person along with all the equipment down there. Atilio was always complaining about bruised arms or knees because he'd reached the wrong direction or dropped something.

Atilio looked up from what he was doing. "Think we got a mouse problem, boss."

Moe blinked.

That had *not* been what he'd been expecting.

"What do you mean?" Moe asked. There couldn't actually be *mice* on board *Aisha*, could there be?

He'd heard of ships being infested before. Even known some pilots who kept cats as a deterrent. His cargo was generally clean, though. Not food. Where in the name of all the stars had they picked up a mouse?

Atilio turned his attention back to the bolt at hand. "Maybe not just one mouse. Probably two, from the sounds I heard."

"So you heard mice, uhm, scampering?" Moe said. Wasn't that what mice did?

"Not quite. Gotcha!" Atilio said as the bolt finally started turning and he was able to twist the wrench easily.

Moe waited while Atilio worked. Tuning the engines was the most important thing his second in command could be doing.

"I noticed that some of the canisters in the kitchen area were out of place," Atilio said.

"Could have been the goons," Moe said.

Atilio flashed him a smile before setting to work on the next bolt. "That's what I thought. But one of the goons accused another of them for getting into their special protein bars. Have you ever tried one of those? They taste like baked tar." Atilio shuddered. "Anyway. I believe the guy when he says he didn't take it. Which means something else did."

Moe nodded. That made sense. However, wouldn't Atilio have found other evidence, though? Like mouse poop? Or gnawed wires?

"So I went looking. Kept my eyes open. Went back to the flitter, where the storage containers are. Heard someone talking. Maybe two someones, as they seemed to be asking questions and waiting for a response. But when I got back there, I didn't see anyone."

"Okay," Moe said. He knew Atilio liked to tell stories, so he bit down on his own impatience and let his friend continue at his own pace.

"Now, it couldn't have been one of the goons in the flitter. But they were all in the kitchen area, eating. As usual," Atilio said. He turned to look up at Moe. "I think a mouse, or mice, *stowed away* aboard the flitter while we were on Niani."

"I see," Moe said. There had been that one life sign that the flitter had reported when they'd first landed, that had disappeared before they'd taken off.

"The reason I asked you to come back here to tell you is because I don't trust the goons," Atilio said, turning deadly serious. "I don't know if those mice are friendly or hostile."

"Why would they be hostile!?" Moe asked.

"Because wouldn't it be easier for the ship to have an 'accident' than for Constantine to pay you?" Atilio said.

Moe swallowed against a suddenly dry throat. He hadn't even considered that.

Atilio shook his head and chuckled. "And you say I'm naïve."

As Atilio appeared to be waiting for Moe to say something, Moe finally responded, "So what do I do if I find these mice?"

With a shrug, Atilio turned back to the bolts on his panel. "Me? I'd shoot 'em with a stunner. Tie 'em up. Then, if they didn't have good answers to my questions, I'd space 'em."

Moe nodded, dread sinking deep into his gut.

He'd threatened to space people before. Had never followed through on it. He wasn't *that guy*.

Then again, before now, he'd always carried legitimate cargo. He carried a laser gun when necessary, when he landed on planets in the Allied Worlds where everyone was armed. He trained with it, and was a fairly decent shot. However, it was always set to stun.

He'd been in a couple of scuff ups. Had stunned one—no, two—people before.

Could he actually force someone out of an airlock? Kill them in cold blood?

Moe took a deep breath.

If the question was his, Atilio's, and *Aisha*'s continued existence, then yes, he could.

"I'll find the mice. And deal with them," he promised Atilio.

"Good," Atilio said. "I'll get us back up into hyperspace in maybe two, three hours. Good hunting," he added.

"Thanks," Moe said.

He went back to his cabin and armed himself with his laser. Then he went out, hunting for Atilio's mice.

Determined not to go home dead.

ELEVEN

Though Rosey had been born on a space station, and spent most of her life in controlled environments, she didn't necessarily hate planets. Sure, she could bitch and moan with the best of them about the foulness of *weather* and such.

However, planets had their own unique appeal. Particularly a place like New Arrakis, which had absolutely awesome, endless sky. It was a particularly cool shade of blue over all that golden and red sand. She could imagine flying through it, dealing with wind and inertia, new challenges to take on.

As well as the heat. That would probably be the trickiest part of building a speedship that flew on this planet. It undulated in waves as it rose up off the sand, creating illusions of water and shade as Rosey drove along a winding one-lane road.

Rosey had done a cursory scan on the statistics for the planet. They didn't really have *spice*, not like how the press releases claimed. Instead, they were solidly supported by tourism, as well as exotic minerals found in some of the mines.

Though Rosey found the notion of an underground hotel interesting, she wasn't intrigued enough to extend her trip.

Besides, if she stayed longer on the planet, the money would end up coming out of her pocket. Jamaal was only paying her for a brief visit, to take a look at this alien ship of his and then tell him it was another J4 knockoff.

The interesting part was where the ship was being held. New Arrakis was a planet in the Kollective, and the ship was in a military yard. That didn't necessarily mean that it was alien— of any of the governments that Rosey had a passing acquaintance with, the Kollective was probably the most stupid and the most stuck in its ways.

According to Jamaal, they, too, had been fooled by a J4 ship more than once.

Rosey was in a self-driving car that took her from the spaceport where she'd landed the little flitter to the military base.

(Dennis had provided enough color commentary about the dust in the air and the grit the flitter was practically *rolling* in that Rosey had finally told him to shut up and to not speak to her again while she was on the planet.)

(She wasn't regretting that decision, sitting all alone in the car with nothing to do and no one to talk with.)

(No. Really.)

The car was small and basic, a two-seater electric, with maybe a top puttering speed of forty miles per hour. She wasn't about to escape in this thing if something went wrong.

She'd just have to steal a military vehicle, if that turned out to be the case.

The military "base" appeared to be a large gray-green Quonset hut stuck out in the middle of nowhere. It was a couple of stories high in the middle of the arch, and maybe fifty yards long.

There wasn't even a fence around it.

The plain did stretch out flat for miles on all sides. There wasn't any way to sneak up on the place. Even on foot it would probably be tricky, given the number of cameras she noted facing every direction on a line down the sides of the building and across the front.

The car pulled up just outside of the front door. There were four parking spots, with only one currently occupied.

Rosey might have a better chance of getting away in the self-driving car at that, given how beat-up and ragged the other vehicle looked. Then again, she knew better than to judge an engine by its hood. Maybe there was something special inside that piece of junk, though she doubted it.

Okay, so maybe Rosey was going to change her opinion of planets in general, and New Arrakis specifically, when she stepped out of her little car.

It was *hot*. Like, sauna hot. Like instantly bake your lungs, sweat immediately pouring from every inch of your body hot.

Rosey grabbed her bag and hurried the few feet from the parking lot to the entrance of the Quonset hut, her short-sleeved blue shirt and shorts getting completely drenched in just that few moments.

Blessed cool air blasted her when she stepped inside. She took a moment, catching her breath.

She heard someone chuckling to her right side. "Not from around here, are ye?"

Rosey turned.

An older gentleman sat behind a desk that took up most of the right side of the front of the building. He was skeletal, all the flesh pulled tight across his long, bald skull. His faded eyes stared curiously at her. Instead of a military outfit, he was wearing a casual, short-sleeved beige shirt, with a black badge clipped to the front left pocket.

Mitch, it said. Contractor.

The old metal desk was pretty bare, with a tablet obviously used for visitors to sign in, and a second tablet that Mitch had been watching something on. Even from where she was standing, Rosey could tell that it was showing some sort of lurid video.

Then again, what else were you supposed to do when stuck out in the middle of nowhere in a dead-end position?

A corrugated metal wall hid the rest of the hut from the front office. A couple of local calendars hung from it, plus a Kollective military recruitment poster, along with a plastic plant hanging from a shelf that held ancient tourist guides. What looked like a wooden door stood in the center of the wall. Rosey was pretty sure it was solid metal, and the lock would hold up against a casual intruder.

Or at least she hoped that was the case, and that this place wasn't really as insecure as it looked.

"I'm here to investigate property number 8375609," Rosey said in what she hoped was an adequately disinterested tone. No need to get anyone's hopes up, just another contractor doing their routine job.

She pulled the credentials that Jamaal had provided for her from her bag and showed them to Mitch. He rose in her estimation because he at least scanned her papers, verifying that she was indeed scheduled to be out there that morning.

Mitch consulted what appeared to be an inventory on a paper—*paper!*—sheet, attached to a clipboard.

"So yer here to see that wreck, huh?" he asked, a bit too interested for Rosey's taste.

Rosey sighed, again trying to deflect any investigation into her or what she was doing.

"They just want me to look at the metals in it," she said, digging out the handheld scanner from the bottom of her bag.

It was about a foot long, and easily five inches in diameter, encased in scratched and dented white plastic. The working end of it was a bit wider, made out of black metal, and looked sort of like a hand vacuum. "See whether it goes straight to the reclamation furnace or not."

Rosey had seen more than one speedship crash in her time. Sometimes it made more sense to just melt a ship down to slag rather than try to extract the exotic metal parts beforehand.

"Gotcha. Well, there ain't much there," Mitch drawled.

Rosey nodded. "So I heard," she said, though that wasn't what she'd heard *at all*. Jamaal had kept talking about this alien ship. Not an alien wreck.

"Come on. I'll show you where it is," Mitch said.

"You don't have to bother with that," Rosey said. She knew that Mitch was just looking for something to do, as currently, she was probably the most entertaining thing on this entire base.

"Suit yerself," Mitch said, reaching for the tablet to resume watching whatever show she'd interrupted.

The one with the bombs paused in mid-explosion.

"Everything's tagged and numbered," Mitch said. "Yer wreck is at the back on the right side."

"Thanks," Rosey said.

Mitch pressed a button on the underside of his desk and the door clicked open.

"I won't be too long," Rosey added as she slipped through.

She wasn't certain what Mitch said as she left. Possibly something along the lines of, "If you find it."

When the automatic lights came on, Rosey understood what Mitch had meant.

This place was *huge*. She hadn't really gotten an accurate sense of how big it had been from the front. She'd thought maybe only fifty yards long, but now, it seemed twice that big.

And stuffed to the gills with storage containers, boxes filled with scraps of metal and parts, shelves covered with engines that looked as though they'd literally been torn out of their compartments, and hulking wrecks of ships.

Why in heaven's name was the Kollective military keeping all this junk? What did they want with any of this? Did they really expect to come back and use any of this someday?

Or was it just in the nature of the Kollective to hoard everything they came across, whether it was broken or not?

Grimly, Rosey made her way through the carcasses of former spaceships, a rack of doors from little cars like the one that had brought her here, as well as a section that she hoped she had time to go through later, as it held a large collection of tools. Broken, but antique. Perhaps something there would be worth stealing and selling.

Not that she'd seriously consider doing that. Every item in here was probably injected with an Intergalactic Tracking Tag. The ITTs worked on every planet, due to agreements signed between the three governments.

If you stole an item with an ITT that was activated, it would start pinging whatever network it found. Unless you kept it boxed into some sort of dead zone, eventually, it would get a message to the local authorities, who would then notify the owners.

The item might be destroyed by the time the message got through, but investigations would be started, and insurance companies might get involved, and whoever had taken the item in the first place had better be prepared to move shop, as they'd not be able to bring stolen, tagged goods to the same place twice.

Rosey passed by the "ship" she was supposed to investigate twice before she finally circled back and took a good look at it.

It was a wreck, all right. All that remained was what looked like a single frame of a ship, a piece that had probably contained the cockpit. Whatever plates or shielding had covered the frame had long since been shredded, based on the delicate lines that went down the sides, almost like someone had drawn them using a black marker.

At least that told Rosey what had happened to the wreck—someone had spent too much time in hyperspace.

The problem? This ship was tiny. The existing frame was maybe twelve feet long and six feet wide, with the top of it maybe five feet off the ground. The front of it narrowed down, as if the nose was going down into a cone. The back of it was cut off flat, where some sort of tail piece had probably been attached. If Rosey extrapolated based on what she saw, there would only be another couple feet added to the front. Perhaps the back of the ship was huge, but if she based her estimate on designs she was familiar with, it would only be another four or five feet long.

How had a ship this small gotten into hyperspace? Did this piece sit on top of a larger ship, and come off? No one did that sort of construction. Not even J4.

There was no way to tell if it was a J4 design or not. There were no lights to see, no sleek exterior.

Rosey squatted down, examining the base of the wreck. It was rounded, not flat. Four solid risers held it in place.

This piece probably hadn't been sitting on top of another ship. It had probably been flying on its own. Unless it had sat in a cradle? But that didn't make sense.

Which brought Rosey back to the question of how it had gotten into hyperspace.

Rosey snapped a few pictures of the remains, then brought out her scanner and started examining the metal of the frame.

Huh.

Jamaal had said that the metal of the ship (*wreck*, not a ship, damnit Jamaal!) had been what had raised flags in the first place.

Rosey understood why, now. Too many exotic metals had been blended together to make this frame. She'd never seen such a composition before. There were even compounds that her scanner couldn't identify. Didn't mean they were unknown —just that her handheld unit didn't have them in its database.

The size of the ship and the metal composition weren't enough to prove that it was of alien manufacture. Maybe J4 had gone all out. The ship could have been inside of a larger ship that hadn't had enough shielding. That could have been used to create this wreck. The timing would have to be precise, though, to just get those lines and not destroy the piece.

There had to be something else that Rosey could find. Some other clue that would tell her the origin of the wreck.

She put her scanner back in her bag, grabbed hold of the edge of the ship, and tugged, hard.

Good. The risers held, and the frame didn't rock or slide to the side.

With practiced ease, Rosey pulled herself up and into the cockpit of the ship.

There was no pilot's chair. Just bare metal. The console in front of her held holes where dials, buttons, switches might have gone. The pattern of holes wasn't familiar, but Rosey didn't expect it would be. Every designer had their own placement of controls. She took pictures of it anyway.

Back behind the panel, though. Would there be any electronics that might have survived the shredding?

Rosey put away her camera, put on her headlamp, reversed herself (happy once again for her short torso), and pushed herself down, so she was looking underneath and behind the console.

There. A partial electronic board, half melted into place, awaited her.

It took some serious tugging for Rosey to break it loose. Then she crawled back out from under the console and looked at her prize.

Some of the board looked vaguely familiar. Transistors. Copper wires. Melted plastic plugs.

But the other parts...What in the heck were those?

No one used fiber optics on a board. Particularly not with fibers so fine that each one looked like one of her own gray hairs. And those might be bundles of fibers, not individual ones. Plus, the board itself was a very non-standard color. Who made blue boards?

Wait. Was that writing?

Rosey brought the board closer to her eyes, wishing she'd thought to bring a magnifying glass with her.

Those letters weren't Arabic. Or Chinese. Or Korean. Or any other language that Rosey knew.

No.

Those letters were alien.

And so, probably, was this wreck.

TWELVE

Jun had never thought about the complications of hiding on a small starship before.

Particularly not one as tiny, run down, and *ancient* as this one appeared to be.

To get from Niani to Ishiman, the planet where the royal court was located, would have taken Jun most of a day in her starship.

She would bet it would take this ship two or three days. If it didn't break down altogether on the way there, and end up limping into some port.

This meant that she was spending many, *many* more days on the ship than she'd originally anticipated.

Which meant finding food. Water. And facilities.

She was just lucky that her implant wasn't due to be renewed for another couple of years, because dealing with her period on top of everything else would have been just too much.

Fortunately, this wasn't a military ship. For the most part, no one came back to check on the cargo. She'd thought she'd heard someone once, and had hid, but she hadn't seen anyone else while she'd waited.

Then again, she couldn't really see out from her hiding place. With the help of Sano, Jun had located a loose panel and managed to pry it open far enough that she could slip behind it.

At first, she'd tried to stay back behind the panel all the time. However, the space was stifling, dark, and dusty. Plus, she barely had enough room to stand, as the panel pressed up against her front and pipes and ducts pressed behind her. There wasn't even room enough to sit down back there.

So Jun cautiously spent her days in the cargo hold of the small flitter, only creeping out into the rest of the ship at night, when she was pretty sure the crew was sleeping, using the bathroom and sonic cleaning unit (which needed fixing, like everything else) as well as stealing a little bit of food. She'd filled her water bottle frequently, drinking more water in an effort to convince her stomach that it was full.

She couldn't take much food, or she'd be noticed. She'd risked taking one of the protein bars she'd found. It hadn't been worth it. The bar itself tasted like burned rubber. She'd had to drink a lot of water after that, trying unsuccessfully to rinse the taste out of her mouth.

Which led to other issues, and barely being able to wait until the crew slept before using the facilities again.

Still, Jun was feeling quite pleased with herself. She had no idea how many more days they would be stuck traveling, but she had a pretty good routine now.

And more importantly, she'd been making good progress translating the Atoylee papers that she'd taken photos of when the scanner had broken.

That had been the other thing she'd never considered—

how to keep oneself occupied when stowed away. She couldn't use any of the entertainment equipment on the ship. Her tablet was made for work and didn't have any books or videos on it.

Her old teacher, Masai, would have been proud of the way she'd used his teachings, keeping herself calm and focused, particularly when the ship dropped out of hyperspace *again*.

So Jun was completely focused on her tablet and on the translation she'd been working on when she heard someone ask from behind her, "Who are you and what are you doing here?"

Jun practically jumped out of her skin she was so startled. She'd been sitting between two of the storage containers, her cloak on and her back to the door, hoping it would provide enough camouflage for a casual observer to miss her. (Though it was so warm on the ship, she frequently went without it.)

Jun slowly set her tablet onto the deck of the ship and turned her head, looking back through the containers.

The tall, dark-skinned man stood there, the one with such nice black hair. He was dressed in a T-shirt, shorts, and sandals. He'd been the one with the binoculars down on Niani.

He wasn't the captain, was he?

He pointed a laser directly at her.

It looked much more modern than the rest of the ship.

"My name is Jun Ogin," she said distinctly, not going to get into the whole princess thing unless she had to. "I'm a xenolinguist and you stole my notes!"

The man opened his mouth, then closed it again.

Obviously, that hadn't been what he'd been expecting.

"I'm going to stand up now," Jun said. She slowly rose to her feet. At the man's gesture, she came out from behind the storage containers she'd been kinda sorta hiding behind.

"Where's your companion?" the man asked. He'd backed

up and was looking all around the cargo hold, as if expecting someone to jump out at him.

"I don't have a companion. There's no one else here. Just me," Jun said, confused.

The man shook his head. "No. My mechanic said that he heard two people talking. And I'm more inclined to believe him than you."

It took Jun a few moments to figure out what he was asking about. "Ah. Your mechanic heard Sano, my computer," Jun said.

The man's eyes narrowed at her. "I don't believe you. Atilio wouldn't have been fooled by a mere computer voice."

"Sano is a bit more than just a computer," Jun said hurriedly. "She helps me with my papers. She has an impressive database of languages.

"It's true," Sano said, speaking up. She used her regular voice, and not the harsh computer-like tones that she could imitate when asked. "I've been working with Jun on the translation of the latest papers from the Atoylee."

The eyebrows of the man crept up toward his hairline. "Really," he said dryly. "That computer is in your necklace, isn't it?"

Jun was so startled she didn't think to lie. "Yes, it is. How did you know?" Most people took it for what it appeared to be, cheap costume jewelry.

The man just shook his head but didn't say anything for a few moments.

Jun breathed deeply, keeping herself calm as he decided her fate.

He was too cute to do anything bad to her. He had a good soul. She could see that.

"You can't stay here," the man said eventually.

"What?" Jun asked. "Are you going to kill me? Throw me out the airlock?" Had she so misjudged him? Just because he had a nice smile?

"What? No. I don't do that," the man said, startled. "I wouldn't do that to you. I won't hurt you." His voice sounded soft and earnest.

He glanced over his shoulder, then returned his gaze to her. His look had turned grim. "But I can't guarantee your safety down here. I'd like you to come and stay in one of the empty crew cabins."

"All right," Jun said, agreeing. It would be a lot nicer than where she'd been staying! "And what should I call you?"

"Moe," the tall man said with a smile and a twinkle in his eyes. "Just Moe."

"And I take it you're the captain of this vessel?"

"*Aisha*. Aye."

He sounded so proud of his ship. Jun made a mental note to not tell him what a wreck it actually was.

She slid back through the two containers to pick up her tablet and her bag, and showed Moe where she'd been hiding. He merely nodded and said that he'd have Atilio look at securing the panel better.

Jun knew the general layout of the ship. It surprised her when Moe took her up a back corridor that she hadn't explored, into one of the closed-off areas of the ship.

"When we get back to a full crew, these will be occupied," Moe said. He sounded a little apologetic. "In the meantime, you stay here."

The room was dusty, like most of the ship. Normally, ships weren't as dusty as planets. However, the air filtration system in *Aisha* needed a serious overhaul.

It was also pretty bare. A bunk that could be pulled down.

A desk in the corner, with a chair that was attached to the wall but that could be easily pulled out. A sink in the other corner. A small sonic cleansing unit beside it.

Everything seemed gray to Jun: gray metal walls, gray painted bed frame, gray cleansing unit, gray sink.

The only spot of color was the back of the desk, which appeared to be a light brown.

"Thank you," Jun said. And she meant it. Even this gray room was going to be better than sleeping on the floor in the cargo hold. "How long until we get wherever we're going?"

Moe gave her a tight smile. "Atilio says three, maybe four more days. What will you do when you get there?"

"Where exactly is there?" Jun asked.

"Allied Worlds," Moe said, then he shook his head. "The less you know now, the better."

"I'll get in touch with my family," Jun said. "I'm sure we'll figure out some way to get me home."

Moe nodded and said, "I'll come see you later. Bring you some food." He bowed his head slightly, then backed out of the room.

It was only then that Jun realized that he'd never put the laser away. He'd held it the entire time he'd been there, ready to aim and shoot her if she made the wrong move.

And that the door was locked, and she had no way out.

THIRTEEN

Duri knew that technically, she shouldn't take the tablet with the information about the alien wreck home with her. Instead, she should leave it at the office, locked in a supposedly secure vault.

Although *technically* the tablet didn't contain anything that important. The alien wreck hadn't been declared top secret.

Not yet, at any rate.

Still, Duri didn't trust many people. Particularly not the security around her office. While some people considered her important, a threat even, too many didn't.

That was all about to change.

She had her team on the move, about to take possession of the wreck. Even if treasure hunters found it first, they couldn't take the whole thing from her. She was certain of it.

She was going to have her prize. In the meantime, she still had the original official report, something no one else had.

Duri lived alone. She'd had girlfriends as well as boyfriends in the past, but no one had stuck with her. Or perhaps she'd been the one to always walk away when things got too personal, as her younger brother had accused her of once.

No matter.

Duri liked her solitary existence. It allowed her to stay focused on her work, as well as the other things that mattered to her, like her books and her music. She always attended her large, extended family gatherings, though the questions about when she was going to find herself a nice mate and start popping out babies were annoying.

As well as when she was going to quit her department and join a more suitable one.

Even becoming Director hadn't been enough for some of her relatives.

They'd all take back their words once she had her hands on that wreck.

Duri lived in a small two-bedroom house in a suburb close to the Parliament buildings. She took a government-owned, shared self-driving vehicle to and from work every day. It was just easier that way. She always sat in the back, buried in her tablet, while the van puttered from one house to the next, picking up or dropping off people who would probably consider themselves to be her colleagues.

Her house was all on one floor, in part because she'd listened to her aunts complaining about the stairs at their houses once too often. It had a pleasant enough yard that she paid dues to the HOA to maintain for her. Like much of Duri's life, the house was fairly nondescript and ordinary, composed of a solid concrete base that went up to just below the big picture windows in the living room, with siding covering the wooden walls above that. The trim and the concrete were white, the siding beige, and the roof brown.

Duri heated up leftovers that night, had a nice glass of wine with her meal, listened to some neo-classical and read a little before turning in early for the night.

She wore her soft, peach-colored expensive lounging pajamas, the ones made out of a synthetic silk that breathed beautifully and made her feel deliciously decadent. Her bedroom was one of her few indulgences: the architectural marvel that was her mattress, top-of-the-line pillows that held her head snugly, and sheets that cost half as much as the mattress itself and were worth every credit given how perfectly they wore, washed, and felt.

When she finished reading, she put aside the specially designed pillow that she used for resting against. Did she need to get up and use the restroom again? Or could she just go to sleep?

Suddenly, there was a strange noise.

Strange. That almost sounded like a dog barking, though she knew none of her close neighbors had animals. (Though no one had backed her amendment to the HOA rules forbidding them either.) The window next to the bed was open, and she wasn't sure if the noise had come from there or not.

No matter what her parents said, or how paranoid they sometimes got, Duri had never bothered keeping a weapon in her bedroom side table. Sure, she was a woman living alone. However, she lived in a safe suburb. And she also worked for the Kollective. Anyone who bothered her would feel the weight of the entire government baring down on them afterward.

However, that sound had been completely out of place with the calm, peaceful night surrounding her.

Duri wasn't sure what made her reach over and turn out the light. Maybe so she could hear better.

Yes. There *was* a sound.

It wasn't coming from outside, but rather, from *inside* her house.

From her study.

Should she call the police? What if it turned out to be nothing? Maybe one of the nearby neighbors had gotten a dog. Maybe the wind had picked up. Was that the sound of papers being shuffled, or merely leaves in the trees?

She sat in the dark, feeling uncomfortably foolish.

She decided to wait for thirty minutes. Then she'd lie down and go to sleep.

After twenty-five minutes, she heard another noise.

This time, it was in her *bedroom*. At the foot of the bed.

Quick as a shot, Duri reached out and turned on the light.

A shadow stood there.

No.

It was a man, dressed in some sort of camouflage that blended into the shadows completely. He wore a mask over his face. All she could see were his eyes, dark brown, peering out at her.

He seemed as surprised as she was.

"Why are you here? What do you want?" Duri demanded.

The man tensed.

He was about to spring into action.

Dressed as he was, he wasn't about to rape her.

No, he wanted to steal something from her.

What did she have that was important?

The report about the alien wreck!

Duri blindly grabbed the tablet sitting on top of her bedside table. In one fluid motion, she threw it, *hard*, sending it sailing out the open window, like one of those throwing discs her niece was so enamored of.

"And the police will be here in ninety-three seconds," Duri lied as she picked up her phone.

The man stared at her for a moment, glanced out the window, then back at her again.

Yes! She'd guessed right. He had been after the alien wreck.

He tensed again.

Maybe she'd underestimated him, as well as his penchant for violence, as his eyes grew darker.

Then he shivered, shook his head, gave her a sharp nod, and slid out of the room. She heard the front door open and close moments later.

Duri took a deep, shaky breath and sat back against her headboard.

Calling the police would be useless, despite her threat. They didn't have the expertise to deal with someone who was obviously a well-trained infiltrator. There would be no evidence, probably not even a tablet in the yard out back.

Slowly, Duri reached for the second tablet sitting on her end table.

The one that contained all the information for the alien wreck.

She'd managed to distract the intruder by throwing her dedicated reading device out her window. Not her work tablet. And she'd kept his attention on that, instead of on her or her end table.

She hadn't realized that the other alien hunters were getting that desperate.

It made her doubly glad that she hadn't bothered locking the tablet in the supposedly secure safe at the office. It wouldn't surprise her in the least if security recorded some sort of break-in that night.

But nothing would have been taken.

Duri hugged the tablet to her chest, suddenly giddy.

She'd outwitted whoever that had been.

There was no possible way to send a message to her team, out on New Arrakis, to let them know that competition was coming. Someone who would mount an attack against her in her own home wouldn't hesitate to try to steal the wreck away as well.

She was just going to have to trust that the team she'd hired would be professional and do their jobs. She'd also double the security at the spaceport, where the ship containing her wreck would be landing.

In the morning, Duri was going to spend some serious time reviewing the names of people who'd arrived on planet in the last forty-eight hours.

The infiltrator had made one mistake. He might have made others as well.

She'd get his name.

Then she'd pursue him with the same fervor she did everything else.

FOURTEEN

Rosey sat, breathing hard, as she stared at the broken electronic panel in her hand.

It was alien. This wreck was alien. It wasn't live contact, but she'd bet that these aliens still lived.

Jamaal was going to be so *unbearably* smug about all of this.

Rosey couldn't wait to go over this wreck with a fine-toothed comb. She was going to spend the rest of the day recording and photographing and cataloguing and—

A hard buzz pulsed against her bonephone. Three times.

Crap.

That was the emergency signal that she'd set up with Dennis.

"Yeah, Dennis, what is it?"

"Oh, so you're speaking to me again?" Dennis asked archly.

"You're the one who sounded the alarm," Rosey pointed out.

"You've got a Kollective military ship headed your direction. And by military, I mean special extraction forces. Ship is from New Rome."

Rosey swore under her breath.

Someone in the Kollective had finally woken up to the fact that this wreck really was alien, and was coming to collect their prize.

"You need to get out of there, boss. Now," Dennis said. He suddenly sounded businesslike, always a bad sign.

"How soon before they land?" Rosey asked as she dove back under the console. What else could she find?

"You've got five minutes tops," Dennis said. "They're flying straight to your location."

Rosey thought hard for a few moments.

All flying vehicles—Human ships, at least—had what was archaically still called a black box. It was actually colored a bright orange, and it contained the flight data recorder and the cockpit voice recorder. Typically, it was located in the area of a ship that was considered the most "hardened," that is, close to the cockpit.

Would aliens follow the same design?

Rosey had no idea, but she bet they might.

She scanned the area above her. Where might it be? If there was one at all, it obviously wasn't directly up, along the top rib.

Were the aliens left-handed or right-handed?

A right-handed black box might be there, but a left-handed one might be just...there.

There was no paint to indicate that this was the black box, or orange, or what have you, but a small device protruded from the rest of the smooth interior. In addition, it had alien letters etched into the metal.

Damn it! She'd left her camera in her bag.

Rosey pulled at the extrusion. Though she was strong, she couldn't just take the whole thing. It was welded on.

"Three minutes, boss."

Rosey put her hand over the device and pushed *up*, hard.

Something gave.

The unit entire depressed slightly.

When she lowered her hand, a whitish square protruded from the center of the device.

It slid out nicely when Rosey grabbed it. It turned out to be a rectangle, about four inches by three inches, and a quarter-inch thick. It was made out of a glowing white material. The smoothness of it felt like glass.

Some sort of crystal matrix? Data storage?

All Rosey knew for certain was that it was alien.

Rosey scrunched herself together and popped out of the alien wreck.

"They're landing, boss," Dennis said.

Jamaal had warned Rosey that her credentials wouldn't stand up to solid scrutiny. And a military extraction team wouldn't give her just a cursory glance.

"Where are they landing?" Rosey asked as she raced toward the front of the Quonset hut, dodging around the accumulated junk.

"Back, behind the building," Dennis said. "That gives you another minute."

"Amateurs," Rosey muttered. They didn't know about how hot this stupid planet was.

Or maybe they did, and they considered it some sort of badge of honor to be able to survive a march across burning sands.

A loud racket from behind her made Rosey pause for a moment, though she knew she was supposed to keep going.

The entire back of the Quonset hut opened up like a door.

Stupid. She should have realized that. There was no way the larger pieces of equipment could have gotten into the storage area through the front room.

"Boss, little skimmer just took off, out of the first ship, heading toward the front door," Dennis warned.

Crap. She was boxed in. Military extraction team on both sides.

Still. That gave her an idea.

"I got this," Rosey told Dennis. "Though you should have the engines on the flitter already hot for when I get there."

Rosey headed toward what was clearly marked as the restroom at the front of the hut, waited precisely two minutes, then sauntered out, walking toward the front door.

Grunts behind her were probably packing up the wreck, while top brass was up front, dealing with the paperwork.

Rosey popped out the door into the office, saying breezily, "Hey, Mitch, just wanted to tell you—oh, didn't know you had company," she said.

Mitch transferred the glare he'd been using on the uniformed dickhead looming over his desk to her.

Dickhead also turned and glared. Some sort of Kollective military jarhead. Rosey barely glanced at him, keeping her attention focused on Mitch.

"Anyway, just wanted you to know that I took a serious dump in your toilet," Rosey said as she kept walking across the office, heading toward the door. "I left the fan running, but you might want to wait until the air cycles through before you step in there."

"Thanks," Mitch said, managing to sound as dry as the desert air around them.

"See you next week, then," Rosey added as she pushed her way out the door.

She was already sweating before that damned planet air sucked every ounce of coolness away.

Though she didn't allow herself to look back, she felt as though she had a bullseye on her back as she hurried to her little rental car.

Only after she was in the car—AC blasting—did she glance at the building. Two additional goons stood on either side of the door, making sure no one came in.

And were probably drowning in their own sweat.

Weren't about to stop someone from coming out. Particularly someone who acted as though they belonged. Would only question someone going in.

Chuckling, Rosey punched in the directions to the spaceport. The little puttering car started its journey back. She composed a message to Jamaal, finally taking a few pictures of her prizes. She wasn't sure when he'd get it, just that he was going to be awfully smug about the fact that yes, even Rosey would certify that this wreck was alien.

And maybe she was feeling a bit smug as well, making her getaway in this ridiculous vehicle.

FIFTEEN

Moe sat in the pilot's chair, running a few searches on the computer as he thought.

Whoever this Jun was, she wasn't a xenolinguist. Or perhaps she was, but she wasn't *just* that. There was a lot more than that to her.

That necklace with the computer in it—it was designed to look like a cheap bauble. It was anything but. It probably contained an AI, or a sliver of an AI's personality.

Only the very, *very* rich could afford that sort of toy.

Moe had seen one before. His cousin's girlfriend had had a copy of something similar made, only to have it stolen almost immediately. It was only then that they'd looked into the design and realized what it was hiding.

He'd never seen someone actually wearing one before.

However, if Jun had such computer power at her fingertips, she could have alerted the authorities where she was, claiming to be kidnapped or something. Any big planet they went toward would have their equivalent of a military.

Allied Worlds didn't have such an organized system. Merely mercenaries who would take the job. Any job. And were difficult to deflect, even if the job got canceled.

Why hadn't Jun sent out a call for help? Had she really just been wanting to find out where the papers were going?

What was to stop her from raising a stink once they landed?

Constantine was going to kill him if she did.

No, Moe was going to have to take the AI necklace away from Jun. And figure out how to turn it off. Possibly just toss it out an airlock. It wasn't a real person, after all.

And maybe Moe was turning into *that guy.*

"Hey boss," Atilio said as he slid into the co-pilot's seat. "You take care of our rodent problem?"

"Yes and no," Moe admitted. He looked down the hallway leading to the kitchen, but he didn't see any of the goons there.

"They're all playing some sort of VR game, together," Atilio said. "Shooting up alien worlds." He rolled his eyes at that.

Moe couldn't help but grin. Not only had Atilio been raised on a planet, he hadn't been raised in a city. He'd actually gone hunting. He'd told stories of having to kill, then clean, his dinner.

These goons—maybe they'd shot people. Or shot at people. More than likely, though, they'd been hired just to look threatening.

"I put our mouse in one of the empty crew rooms," Moe said slowly.

Atilio's eyebrows crept up to the top of his forehead. "Really? Why didn't you space him? And isn't it a them?"

"Just a single her, not him. Jun Ogin. Supposedly a xeno-linguist, who was offended that we stole her notes," Moe said.

"Okay," Atilio said, looking confused. "And you believed her."

Moe nodded. He had. She had a soft look in her eyes that spoke of education. She'd been mussed, and scared, and all he'd wanted to do was to take care of her. Like he would one of his sisters.

Except that none of his relations—no woman he'd ever met —had filled him with such a warm glow.

He still didn't allow himself to trust her, though. She'd been lying to him. He didn't know how he knew, but he did.

While most of the ship didn't have cameras that worked, he'd walked her by one that did, at the back of the ship where no one ever went. (Of course, that would be the location of the single camera that did work.) He'd isolated a picture of her profile, and was now running a comparison on it against important public figures and rich people.

The computer gave a soft ping before Moe could explain more to Atilio.

He brought up the picture he'd taken, along with the matching photo.

"Hot dang," Atilio said. "We got us a princess?"

"Shhhh," Moe said, though he was nodding. He looked from one photo to the other. The computer rated the match at seventy-three percent. However, the biography of *Princess Jun Ogawa* did include the fact that part of her charity work included alien linguistics.

"That's her," Moe said after a few moments. "I'm pretty sure. Yeah. She said her name was Jun, though she gave a different last name."

The photo the computer had pulled up was from some sort of publicity shot of the royal families, at a charity event. Jun was smiling, laughing and talking with someone, eyes animated and warm glow that Moe felt in the center of his chest.

"Smart," Atilio said, though he was shaking his head. "That way she doesn't have to learn a new name to answer to. And the last names are similar enough." He paused then threw a glance toward Moe. "So what are you going to do, boss?"

Moe sighed. "Not sure yet," he said honestly. "Just figured out who she is. Should probably go and talk with her about it."

"We going to ransom her?" Atilio said.

"No, we are not going to ransom her," Moe snarled.

"Would solve a lot of our money worries."

"I'm not *that guy*," Moe said, knowing he was repeating himself.

At least, he wasn't *yet*.

And he didn't want to be that guy, particularly not with Jun.

He sighed and went to the kitchen area to heat up a couple of mugs of tea. The three goons were all still intensely involved with their VR game. He doubted they even noticed his arrival, but just in case, when the tea was ready he ambled to the side, as if going to his cabin before he cut across and made his way to the back of the ship.

The door was programmed to his palm print alone. That would keep the goons out. It also meant that not even Atilio could open the door.

It wasn't that he didn't trust his second in command. That wasn't it at all.

Maybe, just maybe, Moe wanted to keep Jun to himself for a while longer.

The door slid to the side. Moe waited until he saw Jun sitting at the desk before he stepped inside, locking the door behind him.

"I brought you some tea," he said, feeling awkward as he stood next to the door.

"Thanks," Jun said. She looked up from where she was sitting and nodded.

Moe crossed the room and set the mug on the desk while he sort of leaned against the wall. There wasn't another chair in here and he didn't want to sit either on the bunk or the floor.

"So, uh, how's it going?" Moe asked. "Your translation?"

Jun grinned up at him. "The Atoylee definitely had some sort of military base up on their moon," she said. "See, Lawaka is mentioned at least a dozen times in some of the papers we've found. But the strange thing is that in their form of katakana, basically, a phonetic alphabet, they spell out Lawaka sometimes, and other times they refer to the moon using their character language. I'm not sure what the implications are, why they would use one and not the other. Unless maybe one refers to the base on the moon, and the other refers to the moon itself."

She looked very pleased with herself, though Moe honestly hadn't really followed much of what she was talking about. "And why is this important?"

Jun opened her mouth, then shut it again. "I'm not sure how much I should tell you."

"Why is that?" Moe asked, stung.

"Because I don't know what you're doing with my papers," Jun said, her eyes narrowed and anger sparking. "You're obviously going to sell all the artifacts to the richest collector. But the papers, those are more academic. They aren't as important. Unless you're giving them to another university?"

Moe just shook his head. While Jun may be a princess, she was still an academic at heart.

"I didn't want to take the papers. Those were in the white boxes, right?" Moe said.

When Jun nodded, he continued. "I just wanted to grab the artifacts, but the three goons—Constantine's men—overruled me."

"I see," Jun said.

"Like you, I assume that Constantine will sell everything," Moe said. "Including the papers. He's the one who employed me to steal them in the first place."

Jun sighed. "Any way I could get you to delay? Maybe even lose the white boxes? Not turn them over to him?" Jun asked quietly.

"No," Moe said. He sighed. "And I doubt that Constantine will sell them to you. Princess."

Jun looked up sharply at that. She didn't try to deny it, though. "So you know."

"Yeah," Moe said. He sighed. He'd been hoping that he was mistaken, that the computer hadn't returned the right profile.

But it had.

"Does this Constantine know about me?" Jun asked.

"No," Moe said, shaking his head. "I won't tell him, either. Not unless you direct me to."

"Why?" Jun asked, obviously puzzled.

"I'm merely down on my luck," Moe assured her. "Constantine isn't the type of person whom I normally associate with. And I don't like to think what he might do to you."

"I'm worth far more alive than dead," Jun assured Moe. "Still. Thank you." She actually took a sip of her tea and looked thoughtful.

Moe tried not to show the relief he felt at her drinking what he'd prepared for her.

Not that he'd slipped anything into it.

Not yet.

He needed for her to trust him. At least for now.

Later, when he removed that AI necklace, he'd break her trust. And his own wayward heart.

Just one more link of bad luck along the long chain he'd been building.

SIXTEEN

Jamaal sat with his back pressed tight against the warehouse wall as the sun started to rise. The city hadn't started to wake yet, at least this part of it. It would be a while before the truckers and other shipping agents made their way to the warehouses and their offices. Before cargo, such as an alien ship, might be carried through the streets.

He tried to breathe deeply, to calm his nerves. To find that reserve that he always carried with him.

However, the refrain of, *"Stupid, Jamaal. Amateur mistake,"* kept running through his head.

He had made a series of mistakes the previous night, primarily by breaking into Duri's house and treating her as though she had no guile, no resources.

He knew better.

Always treat a target with respect. Every target has unexpected depths. That way, you didn't cut corners.

Like Jamaal had.

Of course, the tablet he'd retrieved from Duri's yard had just been a dedicated reader. It hadn't contained any information. No intelligence to be gathered from it beyond Duri's reading tastes.

Next time, he might not leave Duri breathing.

In the meanwhile, he had a chance to redeem himself, by stealing the alien wreck from her.

Jamaal had originally hired a team to carry out this part. He hadn't planned on accompanying them.

Now, the fight had gotten personal.

And Jamaal wanted the chance to redeem himself, at least in his own eyes.

The team he'd hired had come highly recommended from a friend of a friend in the business. He hadn't met the team leader before now, just done business through secure, anonymous messages. But Floyd had been happy enough to bring Jamaal along. He'd obviously heard something of Jamaal's reputation, so there wasn't that stupid macho posturing that sometimes happened when an outsider joined a mercenary team.

Floyd turned out to be a tall man of some sort of Asian descent, a whisper-thin black goatee serving as the counterpoint for his pointed, shaved skull. He was lean and wiry, and would be a good match for Jamaal based on the way he carried himself. The rest of his team weren't as good, but they were armed to the teeth and ready to commit violence at the drop of a hat.

And sometimes, a job just called for that type of crazy.

The spaceport one block away was on high alert. Jamaal had assumed that would be the case, that Duri would have warned them that someone was coming.

Not that the Kollective military were anything to sneeze at to start with. They weren't as good as the Emperor's troops, of course, but they weren't bad, either.

The rot didn't set in until the upper levels. Lower grunts still were eager to prove themselves.

They'd get their chance today.

The plan was pretty simple.

Jamaal had already located the ship that contained the alien wreck. Once it landed and the cargo got unpacked, it would have to be transported somewhere. Probably to a secret location that Duri had already prepared, knowing that woman.

The most vulnerable time would be after the cargo had left the spaceport and before it got to wherever it was going.

Therefore, Jamaal and the others were waiting just one block away from the spaceport entrance that all trucks used. Floyd assured Jamaal that he had eyes on the inside, so they'd know which of the vehicles leaving the spaceport would be the one to hit.

All the trucks accompanying the cargo would be bombed. Last truck in the convoy first, then the first truck, then they'd work their way toward the center. Once all of the other trucks were disabled, Floyd's people would steal the cargo truck that contained the alien ship, drive it to the location that Jamaal had secured. A flitter was waiting there, warmed up, and would fly into space quickly.

Of course, the alien wreck would already be tagged with an ITT. First thing Jamaal would do once he reached space would be to find the damned tracker and get rid of it. He had special equipment that the most sophisticated thieves didn't, and could find a tracker even if it had been injected into the metal of the ship.

Then he'd have his prize. Duri wasn't about to win this round.

"Coffee's just started," came Floyd's voice over the earpieces that everyone on the team wore. It was the agreed upon signal for when the transport ship had landed and the cargo was being moved from the ship to the nearby trucks. "Pot holds half a dozen cups," he added.

So, six trucks accompanying the main one. A bit of overkill.

However, Duri had reason to be paranoid. Jamaal had given it to her.

Jamaal itched at the blanket draped over his back. While there weren't many itinerate homeless people on the streets of New Rome, there were a few. Enough that Jamaal didn't feel as if he stood out by sitting there on the corner, a bowl in front of him with a couple of coins in it.

The others of Floyd's team were spread out up and down the street, sitting in cars, talking together, one of them even walking what looked like a small French poodle.

Dog might be a killer. Or it might be a decoy. Jamaal wasn't about to get close enough to find out.

A buzzing startled Jamaal out of his funk. He started cursing himself again.

Of all the stupid mistakes.

He'd left his comm on so that someone could *call* him.

The buzz wasn't stopping, either.

That was when Jamaal realized that it hadn't been a mistake. He *had* turned his comm off. The only one who could get through to him was Rosey.

Jamaal looked up and down the street, but nobody was paying any attention to him.

Slowly, he reached inside his pocket and pulled out the comm.

The message was just a bunch of pictures.

Rosie's face appeared, holding what looked like some sort of computer panel next to her head.

The next was a closeup of just the panel.

Rosey had helpfully circled writing on the panel, adding the words, "ALIEN LETTERS!!!" next to it.

Jamaal couldn't contain his small gasp. He eagerly pulled up the next picture.

It contained a small, glowing rectangle. Rosey's commentary said, "Data recorder for the wreck? Control chip? Party favor?"

Jamaal couldn't help but roll his eyes. That was Rosey.

However, it meant that she'd successfully visited the wreck. Had pulled something important from it. Before Duri could get her hands on it.

Now, Duri was going to lose it all.

He sent a quick reply back to Rosey, responding as Jamaal the flamboyant merchant would, "FABULOUS DARLING!" Then he shut his comm down completely. He didn't want to be distracted again.

Things were about to get a little crazy.

When Floyd announced that the coffee was being poured, Jamaal readied himself, waiting for the first trucks in the convoy to pass. He was part of the team taking control of the truck containing the cargo. The others were responsible for bombing the escort.

While Jamaal understood the appeal of blowing shit up, it had never been his preferred method of operation. He'd generally been a "slip in under the radar and knife someone in their sleep" kind of guy.

This morning, that was no longer an option.

The first explosion sent him to his feet, flinging that damned itchy and stinky blanket to the side. He slipped on a helmet, the rest of him already covered in heavy armor. He was armed with guns that used projectiles, which he shot into the wheels of the first truck. Unnecessary, as it suddenly lifted off the street as the missile that had slammed into it exploded upwards.

Before Jamaal could disable the second truck, a stream of Kollective soldiers came racing out of one of the nearby buildings. They hadn't spotted him (yet) but were already shooting at Floyd's team.

Crap. Not only had Duri doubled the number of trucks accompanying the cargo, she'd also sent teams into the nearby buildings, recognizing that this corner was the most vulnerable spot the cargo had to pass by.

Probably had other grunts waiting at every other choke point along the transport's path.

Jamaal had underestimated the woman. Again.

Floyd and his people were about to be slaughtered.

Jamaal was already yelling into the comm as he started shooting Kollective soldiers, knocking them off before they realized they were being hit.

"Mocha! Mocha! Mocha!"

At least Jamaal had thought to come up with some alternative plans in case everything went sideways.

Mocha had always been in response to the very worst possible outcome.

Floyd's voice came on, overriding the other shouts and general chaos.

"Are you sure?"

"Yes, damn it," Jamaal said. He added, because he knew that Floyd's people needed to hear it. "You'll be paid the same anyway." Then he ducked behind a corner, out of direct sight of the Kollective soldiers. He continued to take potshots at any available target.

"You heard the man," Floyd said. "Mocha all the way."

Instead of trying to isolate the truck carrying the alien

wreck, all of Floyd's mercenaries focused their considerable fire power *on* it.

Jamaal wasn't surprised when the first couple of missiles bounced off the hardened sides of the vehicle. Possibly it had some sort of shield generator inside, protecting it.

However, that shield didn't last long.

The next shot got through, blowing up not just the vehicle but everything inside.

Floyd's people were effective. And thorough. And probably enjoying themselves far too much, based on the woops coming through the comm. They kept hammering the truck containing the alien wreck, reducing everything to slag.

Once Jamaal saw that the destruction was well in hand, he said, "I'm going to start another pot," meaning that he was leaving the team.

He raced down the street into an alley, grabbed one of his voluminous orange robes from his backpack, and slipped it on before he reached the end of the passageway.

Once there, he walked peacefully up the sidewalk, calling for a cab to take him to the spaceport from a burner comm, that no one would be able to trace to him.

He hadn't won this round. Not by a long shot.

However, he hadn't lost it either.

He'd call it a draw with Duri.

He just hoped that the piece that Rosey had was as important as he believed it to be.

Or all of this would have been for nothing.

SEVENTEEN

Dennis examined the pieces from the alien wreck that Rosey had found, making all the appropriate "Oh" and "Ah" noises that she required.

He just didn't get the whole thing. Sure, it was from an alien ship. It meant that there was another alien race out there. One that probably had hyperspace capabilities, which neither of the two alien races that Humanity knew about had gotten around to inventing.

However, there were always going to be more aliens out there. It was just a matter of time before Humanity ran across them.

Or they found the Humans.

Rosey had sketched out what she thought the wreck might have looked like before it had been shredded. Conical nose, that she colored a bright red for reasons only known to her. Squared off rear end, with massive engines. She'd added guns, laser cannons, on either side of the cockpit. Again, why she assumed this was a fighter was something only Rosey knew.

Dennis had *no opinion* about it, though. He hadn't seen

the wreck. Rosey's pictures weren't that great (he didn't blame her for that, as she'd thought she'd have more time examining it).

Even the glowing chip wasn't that interesting to him.

He did agree with her that it was some sort of crystal matrix that probably held data. However, she was going to have to redneck together a reader for it. And even if she did manage to figure out how to read the information on the chip, then she'd have to translate it.

Seemed like far too much work for so little reward.

Particularly since that wasn't actual *live contact*. Just another alien race who might be in the process of blowing themselves up.

No, the only thing that Dennis really found intriguing were the readings from Rosey's scanner.

Were those alloys something that she should add to his frame? Something that would protect him better during hyperspace?

He posited that theory to Rosey as she sat in the small eating nook (and really, she should let him add the hologram windows, it would add *so* much ambiance to the space, but that was an argument for another day).

"There are some materials that not only did my scanner not recognize, they aren't common anywhere," Rosey said. "They're pretty exotic, and are never found in combination with the other metals."

"In our known space," Dennis added.

"True," Rosey said. "But I keep thinking that they might be part of an alloy, not natively available."

"What sorts of properties do they have?" Dennis asked.

"I don't know. Nobody's bothered doing much testing on them," Rosey said, taking a sip of her tea, something with herbs to help her sleep that night. Otherwise, she'd be awake and working on things. They were supposed to meet up with Jamaal back on *Lorenzo* the next morning, and she wanted to be fresh, not overly caffeinated and buzzing. Or so she'd tried explaining to Dennis when he'd offered to make her something more flavorful.

"So while we're at the station, how about I order some of those metals for delivery to the workshop? That way you can do some experimenting with them?" Dennis suggested.

He'd already found them in a catalog and was just holding off purchasing them until he had Rosey's approval.

After all, this was coming out of *her* credits, not his decorating budget.

"Sure," Rosey said after a few moments. "I don't have a full lab. But Lloyd owes me a favor or three. I could probably sweet talk him into letting me use his setup."

Lloyd lived on *Lorenzo* and worked as some sort of chemist. Dennis didn't necessarily approve of him. His interest was not limited to Rosey's engineering expertise, but extended to Rosey, herself.

The first time Lloyd had been invited onboard *The Roadrunner* Dennis had found him snooping around. Dennis had alerted Rosey, playing a real-time a video for her, showing Lloyd calmly walking up one of the hallways, trying every single door.

Lloyd had laughed when Rosey had confronted him about it, accepting her accusations of snooping, telling her that he was just curious about not only her ship, but her and her life.

Rosey had unfortunately fallen for it, and Dennis had had to turn off not only his sound but his cameras as well when the pair of them went back to Rosey's private cabin.

He was glad that his programmers had never encouraged him to have *those* sorts of desires.

"Do we have to involve Lloyd?" Dennis asked, pausing and not immediately purchasing the metals in his cart.

"I don't necessarily want to announce to the universe that we have an alien ship wreck, and that we're trying to recreate the metal in it," Rosey said dryly. "Lloyd would easily believe me if I told him I was just experimenting. And I can distract him other ways, too."

"You shouldn't have to do that," Dennis said. "Just find someone else. What about Xi Long?"

"He would be my first choice of metallurgist," Rosey admitted. "However, he's far too curious. I couldn't put him off or distract him. He'd ask too many questions."

"And Lloyd wouldn't?" Dennis said.

Rosey tilted her head from side to side.

Dennis didn't sigh. It was so much easier if Rosey would just speak to him, and vocally communicate everything she was thinking about or feeling. He had studied some Human body language, and he could read Rosey's the best. However, it would never be his forté. He was much better at making someone comfortable in a setting, getting the chairs and colors and lights and ambiance *just so*.

Reading people was just a pain in the ass.

"I think that Lloyd could be dissuaded from asking too many questions," Rosey said slowly. "Distracted."

"What, are you proposing to use sex to drag his focus away from the metal?" Dennis asked, trying not to sound as disgusted as he felt.

"Maybe," Rosey said. The way she was smiling made Dennis wish he had his own head, just so he could shake it.

"Fine," Dennis said. "I don't trust him, though. And I don't think Jamaal will trust him either."

That gave Rosey pause. "Hmmm. That's possible." She thought for a moment. "I don't think Jamaal has met Lloyd. Maybe I should arrange for dinner for the three of us a couple nights from now."

"That sounds like an excellent idea," Dennis said. He finally went ahead and ordered all the materials that made up the alloys of the alien ship.

He just wished that there were more pieces of the ship, something additional to study. Something other than Rosey's little hand scanner report and few snapshots.

Hopefully, Jamaal would be able to figure out a way for them to see whatever reports the Kollective had put together about the wreck.

And maybe Dennis would no longer be able to tease Jamaal about being a Bigfoot hunter.

He'd just have to find something else.

EIGHTEEN

Jun jumped, startled at the buzzing sound that issued from Sato.

"What? What is it?" she said, looking around her tiny cabin.

"You need to stand up and walk around," Sato said severely. "You've been sitting for far too long, your legs are cramping, your eyes are bleary, and your hands are stiff from all the work you've done."

Jun blinked. Everything that Sano said was true. Though she resented the intrusion, she knew she'd feel better if she listened.

Plus, Sano was likely to keep distracting her in increasingly rude ways if she didn't.

With a sigh, Jun pushed away from the desk she'd been working at and stood up. She walked from one side of the room to the other. Four whole steps each direction. She swung her arms as she walked, trying to bring more circulation into her fingertips. Then she stood and rolled her shoulders, this way, that way, reaching down and touching her toes for good measure.

When she reached for her chair, Sano said, "No!" so sharply that Jun flinched.

"Why not?" Jun asked plaintively. She sounded like her youngest niece when being told she couldn't have a second piece of cake for dessert.

"Because you need a longer break," Sano said. "You need to run in place or something to get your heart rate up. Maybe do some pushups."

Jun made a face, but she complied. She knew that Sano was right, that she needed to take a break for a while. She'd been working almost non-stop for the last day or so, spending every waking moment curled over her desk.

However, the puzzle she was picking at was so compelling! She *knew* that she was getting closer to solving it. At least as close as she could get with the limited resources she had on hand.

Her instinct that the aliens had used two different names for the moon in order to indicate a place *on* the moon was probably right. One instance, using the older characters, referred to the planetary body itself. She was ninety-five percent confident that using the other alphabet meant they were referring to a settlement they'd had up there.

The other thing that the papers kept mentioning was a new compound word. If Jun had the base parts right, it translated (roughly) into, "Sunflower Bomb."

While the unenlightened called the Atoylee sunflower people, they weren't. Not really. They did have a plant that was similar to a sunflower, though, that in their poetry they compared themselves to.

Why would they name a bomb after a sunflower? What would it do?

And who had they been fighting?

There were too many words that were spelled out in their version of katakana, too many foreign names that Jun couldn't trace, couldn't find other references to. Knowing how to pronounce the words didn't help. They were still nonsense to her.

Still. She was looking forward to being back in civilization and talking with other scholars about what these words could mean.

Particularly the word *Bukoykan*. It had been referenced often toward the end of the document, and frequently associated with the Sunflower Bomb.

The word Bukoykan had such a foreign flare to it. It wasn't like most of the words in the Atoylee language. It had too many full stops. It was frequently written with their version of hyphens—Bu-koy-kan—which made it even more difficult to translate.

If only the Atoylee had standardized their language! Or had a single alphabet.

Though if she was honest with herself, she wouldn't be as interested if it had been an easy puzzle to master. It was one of the reasons why she studied the Atoylee and not the Huzzomi. Not only was the planet Niani closer to her own home world of Ishmani, the language of the Atoylee was so much more complex. Though the Huzzomi had more than one language, for the most part, it had a single, standardized alphabet, kind of like Humans and English.

Jun was in the middle of her second set of pushups when she heard the door behind her snick open.

Moe stood there with a tray, full of something that smelled delicious.

"Oh. Hi," Jun said, hastily standing up and brushing her hands off on her pants.

"Hi," Moe said, his smile warm and his eyes twinkling.

He looked so cute when he was smiling.

Though when he looked serious, he did have those dreamy brown eyes that made him look like a poet.

"I brought us both some food. I thought we could eat together. Unless you want to get in another set of reps?" he asked, teasing.

Jun didn't normally blush. She'd had too much social training to be easily flustered. From an early age, she'd learned how to present herself to the public. Though she wasn't in the full limelight, she was still an Important Person, and she frequently had cameras (or worse, drone cameras) pointed at her.

However, something about Moe made her cheeks regularly flare red.

"No, I'm good," Jun said. "Sano was being her usual task mistress self, insisting that I get up out of my chair and do some exercise. Instead of just sitting there working."

"Good job, Sano," Moe said.

That made Jun smile even more. Moe had gotten a lot more comfortable around Sano these last few days.

She shook her head.

No. She'd only known Moe for a few days.

It just felt as though they'd been hanging out together for weeks.

He'd brought a second chair in with him after the first time he'd visited her. He'd also given her a small folding table. It didn't make the place luxurious. Nothing short of a complete overhaul, not just to this gray room but to the entire ship would do that.

However, it did make it slightly more comfortable when the pair of them ate together. Moe had been sharing every meal with her, asking how she was doing, letting her ramble—just a bit—about her translation.

Then again, she let him ramble as well, talking about the planets he'd visited, the cargo he'd carried, the strange and wondrous people he'd met.

His life had been so very different than hers, growing up with such a huge family, being the seventh son of a seventh son. Yet, at the same time, she felt as though his family had placed as many expectations on him to do great things as hers had placed on her.

Perhaps all families were like that.

Jun set up the table and the second chair while Moe waited, then he set the table, removing the dishes from the tray. It was a nice touch, making their shared meal more cozy.

Today, Moe had heated up a chicken, rice, and garlic soup. The shelf-stable bread was only slightly rubbery, and he'd liberally slathered a butter-like substance on it, then warmed it in the heater.

Jun missed fresh vegetables, though she wasn't about to say anything about that to Moe. He was doing the best he could with what he had. She was just lucky that he'd packed extra provisions, and that the ship was actually going to arrive at its location soon. Otherwise, she might be stuck eating the burnt-rubber protein bars that were favored by one of the goons.

"How is the translation going?" Moe asked after a few moments.

Jun realized just how starving she'd been, as she'd already inhaled half of the soup he'd given her.

"Really well," Jun said as she forced herself to slow down. She told him about her breakthroughs with the moon, the Sunflower Bomb, and the Bukoykan as she slowed down and tried to actually appreciate her food.

Moe listened and asked a few questions, just to make sure he understood what she was talking about.

"How are repairs going on *Aisha*?" Jun asked.

"We'll be arriving tomorrow morning, early," Moe said. He gave her what looked like a forced smile. "Just one more jump that Atilio says should be easy."

"Good," Jun said. Suddenly, she wasn't hungry any more, and she put the piece of bread she'd been nibbling on down. "What happens then?"

"I turn over all the storage containers to Constantine," Moe said. "I get paid. I make the next bank payment on *Aisha*. And I go searching for more legal cargo."

"I see," Jun said.

"What about you?" Moe asked. "What will you do once we make planetfall?"

Jun sighed. "I'll have to contact my family. Tell them where I am. Get someone to send a ship out to pick me up."

"You don't suppose you could hire someone local to return you back to your home, do you?" Moe asked with a lazy smile.

Jun felt her eyes grow big. "I could do that!" she said. Really, that would solve so many of her problems. Just hire Moe to take her back to Ishiman.

Then she couldn't help but tease. "You wouldn't happen to know anyone I could call, would you? Who would be available for this type of run?"

"Maybe," Moe said, his expression serious but his eyes twinkling. Then he paused. "When would you call your family?"

"After we land?" Jun said, confused by the question.

"Not before?" Moe asked. "You wouldn't try to contact the authorities and get them to stop Constantine from taking and selling the storage containers?"

Jun sighed. She'd thought about that. She really had. She and Sano had discussed it at length.

If she alerted the authorities immediately, she might be able to get this Constantine in trouble. From what little she'd heard of him from Moe, he certainly didn't sound like a nice guy.

However, she hadn't been able to figure out the timing in order to turn Constantine in to the authorities while at the same time protecting Moe.

She could only report Constantine after she (and Moe) were well away from the planet.

"No," Jun said. "I wouldn't call the authorities right away."

"And what about Sano?" Moe said. "She won't start screaming for help as soon as we're in reach of a major planet network?"

"If I had permission to, I certainly would," Sano's dry voice said, joining the conversation. "However, someone's given me *explicit orders* not to. I cannot reach out to *anyone* without her permission."

Jun couldn't help but roll her eyes at Sano's tone. They'd negotiated some—Jun had finally granted that Sano could call for help sooner if it looked as though Constantine was going to be stupid regarding Jun.

"It seems that *someone* has more concern for your safety than for her own," Sano added.

Moe blinked, looking surprised, as if trying to process what Sano was talking about.

"Wait, what, are you trying to protect me?" Moe said.

"Of course. Dufus," Jun said.

No. Why would she say that? She caught herself yawning.

She must have been doing too much work if she was suddenly crashing this way.

"I want you to be safe. And to safely get away. Before I do something to that man Constantine," Jun assured Moe.

Again, what had loosened her tongue so?

She yawned again.

"And Sano, you wouldn't call the authorities either?" Moe said, as if he really needed to hear it again, as if he hadn't believed her the first time.

"I *can't*," Sano replied.

"Don't be bitter," Jun said. "I'll let you order me around to your heart's content once we're back on Ishiman. At least for a while."

Jun blinked and tried focusing on Moe. Why was her vision suddenly fuzzy?

"Though it will probably be a long time before we get back to Ishiman," Jun said. Her voice sounded dreamy, even to her ears. "A long time, with you and me just exploring the galaxy for a while."

"I see," Moe said. He looked sad.

"Don't be sad," Jun said. "You should be happy that we'll have a chance to be together for a while longer. Going back to Ishiman on *Aisha* would be fun."

Moe shook his head. "I doubt you'll feel that way once you wake up."

"What?" Jun felt herself tilting to one side.

Crap. Why was she suddenly on the floor?

"Let's get you up and to bed," Moe said.

"Did you drug me?" Jun asked. Fear spiked through her, clearing her head for a moment.

"Yes," Moe said, with a tight smile. "I was planning on

taking Sano from you. Spacing her. So that you couldn't call the authorities once we landed."

"But I—I wouldn't do that. She won't do that!" Jun complained. She found Moe's arm around her so comforting. Even if he had drugged her. She may have found herself leaning into him. A little.

"I know that, now."

Jun wanted to protest more as Moe tenderly tucked her into her bunk, but words were too hard.

"We'll be there by the time you wake up," he assured her.

Jun's eyes were already closing. She wanted to protest—how could Moe do that to her? Didn't he know that he was special?

Would he take Sano anyway? It wasn't as if she could do anything about it. And poor Sano couldn't either.

Despite her conflicted feelings, Jun felt herself sinking down into sleep.

Maybe she just imagined Moe kissing her forehead softly as she drifted off.

Or maybe she just wished it, hard, as it would probably be the last time she'd ever give him the chance to.

NINETEEN

Duri sat frozen at her desk.

The alien ship was *gone*? Destroyed by enemy fire?

She'd watched the recordings three times before she'd sat back in her chair, unable to comprehend what had just happened.

How could they do that to her?

Surely there would be something left. Maybe she could get scientists to examine the remains and rebuild.

She glanced at the frozen picture on her computer.

No. There was nothing left. The attackers had hit the truck with enough firepower that all the metal had melted. The fire department had had to use special equipment just to get the fire out, as some of the metal on the truck was still burning by the time they got there.

Even if they sorted through the slag, there was no telling which bits of metal came from where.

Duri looked out across her office, her eyes unseeing for a while as the grief settled deep into her bones. She felt numb.

Her assistant poked her head into the office. She asked

something, Duri had snapped at her—what, she didn't remember, it had been automatic—then everything faded again to gray.

Finally, Duri roused herself. She found herself repeating the word, "No," over and over again.

The attack had happened. Someone had destroyed the alien wreck. All she had left were those few initial preliminary reports, held on her air gapped tablet that someone had tried to *steal* last night.

No.

They—whoever they were—were *not* getting away with this.

Duri kept trying to figure out *why* someone would destroy the alien ship. The only reason she could come up with was that they'd gotten to the ship first.

They'd *acquired* something from the wreck. Something important. Something that contained enough information about the aliens that the rest of the ship could be junked— nothing more to learn from it.

Duri had no idea what that item might be. However, it was time to focus the considerable resources of her office toward finding those people.

And making them pay for what they'd done.

Rage suffused Duri, lifted her up. She stoked her anger by watching the recording of the destruction of the alien wreck one more time.

As this had been an attack in broad daylight on a military convoy, Duri didn't have to do much persuading to get a military investigation team assigned to her. While the military would have its own team, reporting directly to General Carrick, this team would report to her.

She wasn't under any delusion that they wouldn't *also*

report to General Carrick and his staff. Still, she intended to get to whoever was behind the destruction of the alien ship first.

And the mercenaries she would hire to go "fetch" the attackers wouldn't have any instructions about bringing people back alive for trial.

The first line of business was to provide her search team with targets to investigate. She knew who to focus them on: the Bigfoot hunters—those people who were just as obsessed with finding the aliens as she was. There were maybe three hundred people she tracked carefully, and another hundred or so she kept tabs on.

Duri called her assistant in. The girl didn't look cowed, or even apologetic. Her dark skin showed no signs of tear tracks. (Duri had fired more than one assistant after she'd made them cry.) In fact, her brown eyes may have had held a touch of anger. She was dressed professionally enough, in a light-blue shirt pulled tight against her curves, a black pencil skirt, and sensible shoes. Cascades of blonde and black braids were pulled together in a large ponytail.

Good.

"What was your name again?" Duri asked.

"Kiley," she replied with a tight smile.

"I had a bit of a shock this morning," Duri said. It was always good to explain when you appeared to be Human to underlings. That way they wouldn't expect it all the time.

"So I heard," Kiley said.

Duri gave her a nod. "But now, we have to find those responsible. I want you to bring me all the files under the heading BF-29627."

"Yes, ma'am," Kiley said, already heading toward the door.

Of course, Duri had electronic versions of all those files.

However, either could get lost, or unscrupulously altered. It was better to have both.

After Kiley returned with the files, as well as with yet another perfect cup of tea (and really, Duri might have to keep Kiley around for a while just because of her ability to do that) Duri started going through the files.

She hadn't ever assumed that the Bigfoot hunters had the wherewithal to mount such a serious attack on the Kollective home world. She'd assumed they were all ineffective.

That had been a mistake. A big one, at that. One that she wasn't about to make a second time.

Carefully, Duri started going through the files, opening up the physical copy, comparing it to the electronic version, then doing searches to find out the current location of the profiled individual.

Two dozen were incarcerated or sentenced to a prison planet—no surprise there.

At least that many were dead. She was going to have to keep her files more up to date.

Dozens were just as feeble as she'd always assumed they were, living on podunk stations or planets, without the means to mount such a fierce attack.

Then there were the others. Ten of them. Who publicly had a lot of credits to their names. A couple of them even appeared to have some military training.

She would focus the professional search team on those ten. Track their whereabouts for the last few days. See if she could get any matches.

She also set up some automatic alerts, looking for people who might purchase the exotic alloys and metals that had made up the alien ship. She didn't have a full report, but she did still have that initial scan done by that incompetent Captain's crew.

If someone decided to replicate the metals in the ship, she'd eventually hear about it.

Duri stood up and stretched after she finished going through the files, trying to find some solace in what she'd accomplished.

She wasn't able to fool herself, though. What she'd done that morning wasn't enough. Nowhere near, actually.

Nothing would be enough, not until she had the head of whoever had *dared* to cross her mounted on her office wall as a warning to all others.

TWENTY

"What do you mean someone destroyed the alien wreck?" Rosey fumed at Jamaal. "Surely the Kollective isn't stupid enough to blow it up?"

There hadn't been enough burnable parts left on the wreck for it to spontaneously combust. None of the metals that she'd examined had been unstable.

Jamaal gave her his patented, casual shrug. "You would think that, wouldn't you?" he said. "All I know is that someone attacked the ship while it was being transported. The entire convoy was destroyed."

"What stupid moron would do that?" Rosey said. They were sitting in her little breakfast nook, the one that Dennis was so proud of (and Rosey had to admit was kinda comfy). However, at this news Rosey found herself up, out of her seat, and pacing around the small kitchen.

"Someone pretty stupid, that's for certain," Jamaal said. "But it doesn't really matter, right? You have the most important part of the ship. Right?"

"Yes. No. I don't know. Maybe," Rosey said. She found herself tugging on her short hair in frustration. "There was still a lot that could have been learned from the wreck."

"True," Jamaal said solemnly. "How much more?"

Rosey stopped pacing and turned to face Jamaal. His tone had gone from casual to serious.

She'd noticed that about him, how Jamaal was a goofball and lackadaisical most of the time. Occasionally, though, she saw this intense foreigner peeking out of Jamaal's eyes.

"I'll never know how much I could have learned, will I?" Rosey snapped back.

Jamaal raised one eyebrow at her.

Rosey sighed and sat back down. "Sorry. It's just such a loss, you know?"

"I agree," Jamaal said.

Rosey shook her head. She'd been teasing Jamaal by not immediately showing him the circuit board and data chip, but now, she didn't want to keep them to herself anymore. They'd just become Important.

Crap.

Rosey sat back down in her seat, then picked up the gold paper bag she'd tied shut with a huge pink ribbon, like it was Jamaal's birthday or something.

And maybe it was, because his eyes grew huge when she placed it on the table in front of him, a grin taking over his face, suddenly making him look younger and a lot less serious.

"This is it?" he asked as he pulled at one end of the big bow that closed the handle of the bag.

"It is," Rosey said. "Both pieces." She'd thought about getting two bags, or maybe half a dozen and fitting them one inside the other, but that would have been too much work.

Jamaal pulled out the board first.

Rosey handed him the magnifying glass she'd brought over from her workshop, wordlessly pointing to the printed letters on the board.

"Oooh," Jamaal said.

Rosey grinned. At least he meant it, unlike Dennis.

"There's writing on a lot of the parts," Rosey said. "Many of what look like circuits. As well as the rubber or whatever that's wrapped around some of the fiber wire."

Jamaal peered at her. "Are any Human boards made with fiber wire like this?"

Rosey shook her head. "I've been checking. Can't find anything like this. Not even J4 goes to these extremes."

Of course, it all still could be some elaborate hoax being played on them. There was no way to verify, particularly not with the wreck completely destroyed.

Rosey just hoped that she was right, and that no one would go to this much effort to fake an alien ship.

"Any idea what it does?" Jamaal asked, tipping toward that serious side of himself again.

"Nope," Rosey said. "If I had to guess, because that's just about all I can do here, I'd say that it wasn't special built. This isn't a bespoke board. Whoever the aliens are, they have manufacturing centers that probably put out thousands of these boards a week."

And that was part of why she didn't think this was a hoax. The parts were too uniform, numbered and organized. It looked like a generic board. There really wasn't any way to figure out what it did.

Jamaal put the board to the side and reached into the bag again, pulling out the chip.

It hadn't lost any of its internal glow. There was something powering it. Rosey had run a Geiger counter across it, but it hadn't registered as radioactive.

"If you look at the bottom, that side, there," Rosey said, indicating one of the shorter ends of the rectangle, "you'll see tiny indentations. Probably where this thing plugged into the device that read it. The device that's now been *blown up*."

Jamaal nodded. "I can just feel the holes," he said as he rubbed a finger against them.

Rosey was impressed. Then again, her hands were pretty beaten up from working on ships all the time. They weren't delicate from just handling merchandise, like Jamaal's.

Jamaal brought the magnifying glass up to the end, examining it carefully. "Are each of these holes the same depth?"

"No," Rosey said, again impressed. "The four in the center are all longer. The one on the side is shorter."

That implied that there was a right way and a wrong way to insert the data chip into its reading device. Probably designed by some engineer who had no idea that you'd be on your back, reaching above your head, if you were doing any maintenance on the ship. A right and wrong way to plug in the chip meant that at least half the time, you were going to get the placement wrong. Depending on the strength of the inserts, you also took a chance of blunting or bending the short one on a regular basis.

It was a stupid design.

However, that made Rosey feel better. It meant that the aliens weren't super-smart, super-advanced, and likely to enslave Humanity when they finally reached each other.

Naw, Humans would probably do something stupid like enslave themselves first.

Particularly if they were dumb enough to blow up the first real alien wreck they'd encountered.

"You don't think it was the aliens, themselves, who blew up the wreck, do you?" Rosey asked. If they were hidden, they might want to remain so. "Some sort of secret, high-powered beam from space?"

"I've heard other people speculate the same," Jamaal said, nodding, though he didn't look up from his examination of the data chip.

Rosey waited. "Well? What do you think happened? Was it Human idiots? Or an alien super weapon?"

"I figure it was some moron," Jamaal said with a grin, finally looking up at her. "It wasn't the smartest move."

Rosey nodded. "So. How do we go about building a reader for this?" That was far beyond her expertise. She could eventually redneck something together. Much quicker, though, to find an expert.

"We?" Jamaal asked, raising that eyebrow again.

"Those parts are mine. Salvaged off a dead ship," Rosey pointed out.

"Stolen, you mean," Jamaal said.

"Whatever," Rosey said, dismissing his comment with a wave of her hand. "They're mine. You're my partner in this. What are *we* going to do with them?"

Jamaal narrowed his eyes at her. "Are you sure?" he asked quietly.

Serious Jamaal was trying to stare a hole through her. Maybe judge her soul.

"Yes, I'm sure. Idiot," Rosey said affectionately. "You think I'm just going to walk away after this?"

"There might be danger," Jamaal warned. He sounded more serious than ever.

Rosey made a rude noise. "What, from idiots who blew up the alien wreck? Trying to keep us away from it? Please."

"Maybe them. But others, too. The Kollective will be coming after you if they ever learn of the existence of these parts," Jamaal said, still with that somber tone that was quite frankly, unsettling.

Rosey took a deep breath, and treated Jamaal's query with the thoughtfulness that it deserved.

"I know these pieces from the alien wreck are important," she said softly. "Since the wreck's been destroyed, they've become Very Important. I'd rather have someone else working on this with me, rather than having to do this on my own."

There. That let Jamaal know that she still considered these items her property, even though he'd sent her to collect them.

Though actually, he'd just sent her to verify whether the wreck was alien or Human. Anything she pulled from the wreck wasn't covered in their initial deal. Something she'd point out to him if he pushed.

Eventually, Jamaal sat back, a smile crossing his face again. "All right. We're in this together."

She was pretty sure that he thought there was an unspoken "for now" at the end of that sentence.

She'd take that as a challenge, should the occasion rise.

"Do you know anyone who can build us a reader?" Rosey asked. Jamaal's network was pretty wide, as was her own. Still, he might know someone he could call on immediately, while Rosey would have to poke and prod and feel out some inventors.

"I know a guy," Jamaal said slowly, nodding. "Oswald."

"Where's he located?" Rosey said. There was something about Jamaal's manner that gave her pause.

"Allied Worlds," Jamaal said. "Planet called Herkules." He

opened his mouth, considered, closed it, then finally said, "Lot of genetic modifications go on there. Oswald has a few."

Rosey just shook her head. The Allied Worlds had this whole Greek mythology thing going with the names of a large number of their planets. The genetic modifications didn't surprise her either.

"Some sort of superman?" she guessed.

"You'll see," Jamaal said with a tight smile.

Rosey just rolled her eyes at that.

Then Rosey told Jamaal about her plans to experiment with the exotic metals her scanner had picked up from the wreck, and asked about having dinner with Lloyd.

"Do you trust him?" Jamaal said. While the question seemed casual enough, the way he looked at her felt judgy. Again.

"I don't," Dennis piped up.

"Dennis is just jealous," Rosey teased.

"Ewww. So not," Dennis assured Jamaal.

Rosey and Dennis explained their reasoning to Jamaal.

"He's distractable," Rosey assured him.

"Let me do some checking," Jamaal said after a few moments of thinking about it. "See whether or not there are any red flags, if he's trustable enough. Or if I can find some other metallurgist who might be better."

"Who won't ask too many questions," Rosey warned.

Jamaal gave her a tight smile. "Not too many questions," he promised.

After Jamaal had gone (leaving behind all the alien parts), Rosey sat for a while, thinking.

She had the feeling that something was off about all of this.

The wreck being destroyed. The increased need for secrecy. The new Importance of the alien parts she'd salvaged.

It had been a game before.

Now, Rosey felt that Jamaal's serious self was going to come more and more into play. Whether or not that was a good thing remained to be seen.

And possibly her own serious, competitive nature as well.

TWENTY-ONE

Moe stood at the door of Jun's room, still conflicted.

Should he just grab Sano and chuck her out an airlock?

Or should he believe Jun that Sano wouldn't start broad-casting an emergency HELP call as soon as they finished their last jump? Not just wouldn't, but couldn't?

And how would Jun feel once she woke up? Would she change her mind?

"Don't do it," Sano warned suddenly.

Moe started. "Why not?"

He wasn't worried about Jun waking up and hearing their conversation. Or remembering it even if she half-heard it. She was too out of it. He'd made sure of that.

No matter how much he hadn't wanted to drug her, how much he hated himself for having done it.

How much he was afraid of turning into *that guy*.

"If you ever want a chance of pursuing this ridiculous romantic course with her, you won't break her trust any more than you already have," Sano said.

"Ridiculous, eh?" Moe said. Though he still felt horrible

about what he'd done, he couldn't help but smile at the thought that Jun liked him. Really liked him.

Then again, she was a princess. He was a failed cargo pilot. Their relationship was doomed from the start.

"Yes, ridiculous," Sano said. She gave a dismissive sniff. "I don't have to go into all the reasons why."

"Which is why I could take you. Space you. It wouldn't matter in the end," Moe said softly.

Sano gave a very Human-like sigh. "I can't argue with that logic," she said. She sounded disgruntled by the fact that a Human was actually making sense, instead of being irrational. "However, I will give you my word as well that I won't immediately alert the authorities when we reach a large enough network."

"How do I trust the word of an AI?" Moe asked reasonably. "I don't know you. You are not beholden to me in the slightest."

The pause was significant. AIs thought at many times the speed of Humans. That Sano didn't immediately have an answer meant something.

What the pause meant, Moe wasn't exactly certain. But certainly something.

"I will not give you any sort of executive command over me," Sano said slowly. "My allegiance is aligned with Jun and Jun alone."

"I know that," Moe said. "And I wouldn't want that, anyway. Just give me some way to trust you."

Sano sighed again. Really, she was quite good at it. Maybe she'd had a lot of reason to sigh, having dealt with Jun since she was a very small child.

That also made Moe smile.

"I cannot allow you to override all my commands," Sano

said. "What I can do is allow you to place a hold on my actions. Not for long. Just a second or so. But you will be able to stop me momentarily, possibly to give you time to get Jun to rescind whatever command she'd just given me. It will be a once-in-a-lifetime, get out of jail free card."

Moe shook his head. He still didn't know if he could trust the AI, if Jun really had instructed Sano to not start screaming to the authorities as soon as they landed.

Yet, just the offer might be enough. That Sano was willing to trust Moe that far.

It might also have given him some hope—just the tiniest amount—that maybe his ridiculous romantic notions weren't completely insane.

"All right," Moe said after a few moments. "I won't space you if you give me such a command."

At least, not now. He made no guarantees that at some future point, it wouldn't be necessary to "lose" Sano.

"See Oh Eee Point Five," Sano said in response.

"See Oh Eee?" Moe inquired. COE? Was it some sort of xenolinguistic tag?

"Comedy of errors," Sano said.

Moe could practically hear the grin in her voice as she continued. "Romantic foolish mortals, the pair of you."

"Thanks," Moe said dryly. "I think."

Before he could talk himself back into what was sure to be a disastrous course of action, Moe left Jun's room, locking it behind him, and went back to the main helm, sitting down in the pilot's chair.

The countdown clock said their next jump was three hours away. They'd be in hyperspace for about twenty minutes. Then it would be another four hours to make it to Psykee.

It didn't surprise Moe when Atilio came and sat down in the co-pilot's chair just a few minutes later.

"So how'd it go?" Atilio said, looking ahead at the stars that shone in front of them. Once they reached hyperspace, the stars would start to stream by. For now, they were moving slowly enough that they appeared locked in place.

Moe sighed. He couldn't help it. "I didn't do it," he said softly.

"I know that," Atilio said, sounding exasperated. He still didn't look at Moe. "What I want to know is why."

"Jun told me that she'd ordered Sano to not yell for help as soon as they reached a big enough system," Moe said.

That finally made Atilio look at Moe. "And you believed her?"

"Jun said she was trying to protect me. And yes, I do believe her," Moe said, lifting his chin up stubbornly.

Atilio shook his head. "You're risking a lot on just the word of a princess."

That sounded more like a warning than a comment.

"I know," Moe said. "I know I'm endangering both of us by not spacing Sano. But I talked with the AI as well. She also gave her word that she wouldn't immediately call the authorities."

Atilio actually rolled his eyes at that one. "You're the boss," was his only reply.

"Yeah," Moe said. "I'm the one who gets paid the big bucks."

That at least made Atilio smile. Moe was always broke because he rarely paid himself anything. Barely enough to live on, always sinking the rest back into *Aisha* to keep her running.

"So what are we going to do with them?" Atilio asked.

"We are going to take the flitter down to Psykee," Moe said

seriously. "With the goons and the cargo. Leave *Aisha* in orbit, with Jun and Sano."

Atilio looked thoughtful for a moment. "You know," he said slowly, "I could put a special lock on the cargo doors, so that they'll only open when the flitter's nearby."

"Really? We have the equipment to do that?" Moe asked, surprised.

"Yeah, well, I've been saving it for something special," Atilio said defensively, running a hand through his curls.

It was only then that Moe noticed just how tense and pale Atilio looked. He'd been working pretty much non-stop since they'd left Psykee, first getting them to Niani, and now back again.

"We're going to make a lot of credits, and I mean a whole lot, once we offload this cargo," Moe said. "And I might have already arranged our next trip. Carrying Jun back to Ishiman."

That just earned him a *look.*

"What?" Moe said.

Atilio grinned at him. "You're the boss." Then he gave a jaw-cracking yawn.

"Go to your bunk. Sleep for the next three hours," Moe ordered. "I'll make sure you're awake for the next jump."

Atilio nodded, suddenly deflating. "Yes, boss," he said, though he didn't sound angry at the command.

After Atilio had gone, Moe tried not to think of all the ways that this could go sideways. Instead, he tried to focus, for once, on the future. Because after the run to Ishiman, things were sure to pick up.

He could regain his place as a legitimate cargo captain. Pick up some more lucrative hauls. Have some good luck again.

Right?

TWENTY-TWO

Jamaal had reached out to Oswald before he'd actually touched the alien data chip, just from the pictures Rosey had sent. It sometimes took a few days for Oswald to reply to a message. Frequently, that was due to the hacker having more delicate fine-tuning of his complicated bio-system done.

Finally, though, Oswald sent a message that he'd be available in a few days' time, and of course, he'd love to see Jamaal and would be happy to work on whatever Jamaal brought to him.

It was a little odd that the message was just text and not video. Then again, who knew what Oswald looked like these days? If he was corpulent or skinny? Maybe he wanted to save his appearance as a surprise for his old business acquaintance.

While many of Jamaal's contacts were on the legitimate side of things, connected to or associated with his work for the Emperor, he'd also developed a few who were definitely not, Oswald being one of those.

Whenever Jamaal needed a special device, Oswald was who he always went to. Oswald worked as an independent contractor, not on the payroll of any of the various warlords, dictators, or other hooligans of the Allied Worlds.

In the early days, if any government or agency tried to bother Oswald or compel his allegiance, he'd just move to a different planet. His operation was completely self-contained.

He'd been on Herkules for a while, though. Seemed the powers that be had finally learned their lesson.

Particularly after Oswald had unleashed a couple of virulent computer viruses on the planet he'd just left, wiping out what little government files and computers there were, as well as messing up all shipping routes.

That afternoon, Jamaal sat at his computer in his bedroom on *Lorenzo*. While he paid for extra rooms for his plants and his workouts, he didn't bother with a separate office. The monitor was built into the desk, and folded flat when he didn't need it. It projected a keyboard for him to type on when it was raised up. The chair was extra comfortable and supportive. It was also strong enough to hold both him and Harkeen when they'd decided to get adventurous.

Jamaal hadn't frequently used a computer when he'd been working. Most of the time he'd been in the field. Now that he was retired, he did spend a little more time on the network, ordering supplies and things, but not much. He preferred working with people, not machines.

That being said, his computer was state of the art, particularly when it came to security. Only he could unlock it, using retina- and other bio-scans. However, just unlocking it wasn't enough: Jamaal had subdivided his computer, and each area was only accessible via password and thumbprint.

Before Jamaal could start doing a deep dive on this Lloyd person, he received an incoming message.

This one did have a recording attached. And it was from Emma.

Jamaal's first instinct was to snap to attention and immediately hit receive and play.

Instead, he made himself sit back and consider the implications of his old handler contacting him out of the blue.

Had she heard about the debacle on New Rome? Had the Kollective linked it to him? Was this a warning from his former employers to knock it off?

Or was this something else? Were they calling him back into the field?

Did he want to go back? Under what circumstances would he return? If any?

For the first year of Jamaal's retirement, he hadn't felt any regrets about his decision. He'd primarily felt relief, as well as an expansion of his soul (something he had only admitted to Harkeen in the dead of night). He didn't have to be so compressed anymore, so on edge, so knife sharp and ready.

He hadn't started missing it until the second year. He'd done a few missions at that point, one-off sort of "fix it" jobs. Enough that he'd felt as though he still had his hand in things and was maintaining his skill set to some degree.

He'd also met Rosey that year, and had gotten to know her rather well. Having a true friend, someone whose company he enjoyed, had helped. He'd made a few other friends that year, though he liked Rosey the best.

She never asked him to be anything other than Jamaal the trader. As far as he knew, she didn't suspect him of having had a serious career other than that.

He knew that as they continued to pursue the aliens, that would probably change, and she'd figure out more of the truth.

Fortunately, he also knew that Rosey wouldn't care. She wouldn't feel betrayed by not knowing. Instead, she'd probably ask him to help her break into places, to steal ship plans or something.

He could count on Rosey to find new ways to use his talents.

However, Emma...Emma knew all about him. Had probably been keeping tabs on him, even though he was officially in retirement.

What did she want?

Finally, Jamaal hit play.

The colors of the Empire filled the screen—gold and green—along with the Emperor's symbol, a pink lotus flower sitting on top of black, crossed katanas. Then came the usual TOP SECRET warnings and dire statements about not sharing the information, etc.

Emma came on the screen. She looked the same as she always did, a petite Asian woman with very short black hair and piercing black eyes. Jamaal had seen her go under-cover more than once, looking (and acting) like a delicate flower.

She could still kick Jamaal's ass six ways from Sunday. He respected her tremendously, though he'd never been friends with her. He hadn't been friends with anyone, really. Something he didn't like to dwell on.

Instead of greeting Jamaal personally, Emma opened with, "This message is going to all active and recently inactive operatives."

Jamaal was so stunned he hit pause before he allowed Emma to continue.

He found himself taking a deep breath, probably the first since he'd seen the message had arrived.

Emma wasn't calling *him* to take care of the situation. It

must be pretty bad if they were calling on not just active but former operatives.

However, she didn't expect Jamaal to have to solve whatever the situation was.

The amount of relief he felt surprised him.

He ignored the fact that just a tiny, *tiny* bit of him was also disappointed.

He hit play and let the message continue.

"Princess Jun Ogawa is currently missing, presumed kidnapped," Emma continued, her image replaced with a picture of a youngish woman, probably in her twenties, bearing a striking resemblance to the Crown Princess Yumi, with her straight black hair and round face.

"Her last known whereabouts was the planet Niani," Emma continued in the background, "where she was part of the Empire's archaeological dig. Her spaceship was found in orbit there. All the finds from the dig were stolen. We presume whoever took them also has Princess Jun. However, we haven't received a ransom note."

That was bad. Either the pirates, or whoever, didn't understand what it was that they had, or they'd already killed her.

Or worse, had put her into *service*.

Jamaal knew the types of individuals who would find taking a princess their ultimate power ride.

He found himself growling quietly.

"Please work whatever contacts you may have to find Princess Jun," Emma said, the picture of the princess replaced with her again. "Quietly," she emphasized.

Jamaal found himself nodding. Yes, something like this needed to be kept quiet. The court must be really worried if they were doing this level of outreach.

"Contact me *immediately* if you hear anything," Emma

warned. "Do not handle this on your own. Let the Empire choose its retribution."

Again, Jamaal nodded. By keeping the rescue in house as it were, Emma was making sure that word wouldn't get out.

Plus, if the princess had been taken, whoever had done it would not only die, their entire network would be destroyed.

As far as Jamaal knew, no one had ever successfully kidnapped one of the royal family, though Princess Jun was just a *Hime*, and not in direct line for the throne.

"Thank you," Emma said, closing her message. "The Empire appreciates your attention to this delicate matter."

Jamaal acknowledged and affirmed that he'd received the message, had listened to it, and would heed its contents before shutting off his computer.

The problem with a princess gone missing was that it was a pretty big universe. It was easy for people to go missing. No one had developed an ITT system for them.

Yet—Jamaal replayed the part of the message that had pictures of Princess Jun in them.

Yes, she was wearing a governess. She had an AI with her. Which was, in some ways, better than a bodyguard.

Had the kidnappers removed the AI? Gotten rid of it so that it couldn't call for help?

Or was there something else going on? Had Princess Jun run away from the royal family?

Jamaal didn't know. He did linger for a moment on her picture. What had she been doing on Niani? It took him just a few moments to discover that she was a xenolinguist.

Hmmm. Something to consider. Later.

For now, he had more important things to find at this point, instead of spending his time searching for a spoiled princess.

No, he was going to find the aliens who were out there.

TWENTY-THREE

Jun awoke with her mouth dry, her head pounding, and a deep rage filling her.

She didn't remember all the details of the previous evening. She didn't need to. All she needed to recall was that Moe hadn't trusted her. He'd *drugged* her.

Then her hand felt for the familiar necklace around her neck.

Sano was still there, and surprisingly silent.

"You there?" Jun managed to croak out after a few moments of swallowing and getting some moisture back into her mouth.

"I am," Sano said. "How are you feeling?"

"Groggy. Headachy," Jun said. She made herself sit up.

The room spun and she shut her eyes, but she didn't allow herself to lie back down.

"There's a box of juice on your desk," Sano said. Her words still sounded clipped. "As well as a message."

Jun took a deep breath, finding her way back into her body before she finally pushed herself to standing.

The room spun slightly, but not as badly as it had when she'd first sat up.

It was just a few steps to the desk chair. Jun felt as though she were pushing through gravity that was three times normal before she got there and collapsed into the seat.

As Sano had promised, there was a carton of apple juice sitting there. Not fresh, of course: it was made from concentrate, with added sugars.

Jun made a face but still drank it all. She immediately felt better. A small covered dish was there, filled with more of the chicken and garlic soup that she'd eaten the night before. She fell onto that, slurping down half of it before she remembered that the last bowl of this soup that she'd eaten had been drugged.

Too late now. She still finished what was there. She also considered licking the bottom of it, even though that went against all the Princess Rules she'd had drilled into her head since she was a child.

Mostly, she still followed them. Particularly when she was in public.

She'd learned, though, that they didn't matter as much in private. And after she'd had Sano reprogrammed, no one bothered her about them as much. Sano still tried now and again.

Jun left the bowl on her desk unlicked as she reached for the recording device. It was a small disk that fit comfortably into the palm of her hand, made out of gray, dingy metal. It looked similar to a makeup compact. However, when she opened it, the lid had a screen instead of a mirror, and the base had buttons, not powder.

Jun put the device back on the desk and pressed play. That way, she wouldn't be tempted to throw it across the room until after she'd listened to the entire message.

She made no promises about whether or not the recorder would survive after that.

Moe's face appeared on the screen. He looked worried.

At least the first thing he said was, "I'm sorry. I shouldn't have drugged you. But I didn't know how you felt. I didn't know if I could trust you or not."

Jun shook her head. Stupid boy. Should have *asked* her instead of drugging her.

"But I am trusting you now," Moe said. His eyes stared soulfully into the camera.

"The door to your room is unlocked," he continued. "You're currently in orbit above the planet Psykee. I'm leaving you up on *Aisha* not because I don't trust you, but because I don't trust Constantine. I don't know if I can protect you down on the planet. So I'm leaving you up here, where it's safe. Or at least safer."

He gave her a grin at that. "Atilio assures me that *Aisha* is stable. At least for now."

Jun couldn't help but grin back. She hadn't spent any time with Atilio, but Moe had talked about him often enough that she felt as though she knew the second in command.

Moe grew somber again. "There's enough food to last you for five days. It's pretty boring food, I'll admit, but it should be enough. Constantine has agreed to see us right away, so I'm hoping to get back up there in the flitter after only a day and a half. If something goes wrong though, well, I've left everything wide open for you. Unlocked. Even if you can't pilot the ship yourself, I'm sure Sano can."

Jun nodded. Though she didn't have any experience, Sano would be more than up to the task. Even with an ancient derelict like *Aisha*.

"You know I'll come back for you. And *Aisha*," Moe said

softly. "So you will see me again, even if it's just to order me to take you directly back down to the planet so you can find another ship to take you to Ishiman."

With a sigh, Jun reached forward and paused the recording. She didn't know what she wanted, not at that moment. She suspected he was correct, though.

She wasn't ever going to trust him enough. Not after what he'd done.

After a few moments of letting her heart be sad, Jun pressed play again.

"Atilio has reconfigured the airlock for *Aisha*," Moe continued. "He swears that the only ship that can access the docking bay is our flitter. Anyone else will have a lot of locks to hack. So if you call for help, be sure to tell them that. You may have to do a spacewalk or something if you decide to leave before I come back."

That surprised Jun. She hadn't expected Moe to have access to that sort of technology.

Then again, she suspected that the only reason *Aisha* was still capable of flying was because Atilio babied her.

Moe looked down for a moment, running his fingers through his hair.

Jun couldn't help but smile, as he'd accidentally left part of it sticking up.

"I'm sorry," Moe said again as he looked up again, his eyes seeming to pierce Jun's soul. "I will try everything that I know to make it up to you. I promise."

The recording ended there.

Jun's anger simmered in her gut. What Moe had done was *wrong*.

He appeared truly sorry for what he'd done.

Was it enough?

Jun didn't know. Probably wouldn't know until after she saw Moe again in person.

With that decided, she refreshed herself, then let herself out of her bunk and went to explore the ship fully.

All the doors opened to her touch. Even Moe's private cabin.

It didn't surprise her that his cabin was full of the color that the rest of *Aisha* didn't have. Little prayer flags done in dark orange and red were strung across the ceiling, with yellow suns and moons as decoration. Swaths of soft fabric hung down on two of the walls, each done in batik with patterns of green, blue, yellow and black. The sheets on his bunk were a deep purple color, with white paisley patterns dancing across them, and a dark blue blanket with stars was neatly folded at the foot of it.

The entire cabin looked cozy, despite all the colors. Or maybe because of them.

Jun didn't pry further, didn't spend time examining the pictures in the frame that kept putting up new ones. She assumed that the few that she did see were his family, all of them black-haired with white teeth shining against dark skin.

Moe had told her that he was the seventh son of a seventh son, and that he had two sisters as well. So much family and obligations, though different than hers.

Atilio's cabin was also open, which surprised her. She didn't even cross the threshold there, but stood in the doorway. It was neat and clean, with schematics taped to the walls and the faint odor of machine oil lingering. The sheets on his bed were tucked in tightly, the folds military-precise. There was nothing personal in the room. She recognized the bag tied to the foot of the bed—a bug-out bag, so that Atilio could leave with everything he needed at the drop of a hat.

That told Jun more about Atilio than she'd known. Did Moe even realize that his second in command had at one point been in the imperial military?

The rest of the ship held no surprises for Jun. She did spend a little time back in engineering, peering down the hatch at the engines below.

"Thinking of sabotage?" Sano asked. She'd been surprisingly quiet during all of Jun's explorations.

"No," Jun said, surprised that Sano would even suggest it. "Just wanting to see how bad it is."

Though she couldn't honestly tell. The engines, what she could see of them from up above, appeared to be running smoothly, all the gauges and dials reading normal.

Eventually, Jun made her way up to the helm, sitting in Moe's pilot chair.

"Do you want to call for help?" Sano said. She sounded almost mechanical, as if trying to keep her voice carefully neutral.

"No," Jun said. "I can wait."

And so she did, for an entire day, entertaining herself with her translations, getting up when Sano prompted her to exercise or eat, or even go to sleep.

A beeping noise interrupted her early in the morning of the second day.

"The flitter is returning," Sano announced.

"Good," Jun said. She walked back to the cargo area and stood outside the door of the bay, waiting for the flitter to dock.

Once the all clear sounded, Jun went into the cargo bay and waited impatiently for the flitter to release its passengers.

However, instead of Moe walking down the ramp, one of

the goons appeared. The other two followed immediately behind him.

"Well, looky what we have here!" he said, giving her an appraising look.

This was Not Good.

Not Good At All.

TWENTY-FOUR

Dennis was sad that Jamaal had given Lloyd the A-Okay.

It meant having to deal with him on *The Roadrunner*.

Which was not A-Okay. Not at all.

Lloyd the Lounge Lizard (or so Dennis had tagged him, along with specific programming so that he would never accidentally use that name with Rosey) was not a fine specimen of Human. Sure, he was tall. Probably just over six feet, which was Rosey's preference. He had a ruddy complexion, which Rosey swore was natural, and not from him drinking too much. (Dennis would just have to take her word on that, because *his* searches showed that at least sixty percent of the time, that big of a nose came from alcohol abuse.) Dennis sort of, kind of, saw the appeal of Lloyd's blond curls, though from a design standpoint, they needed brushing or product or *something* at least half the time.

Honestly, Lloyd was more lumberjack than slinky lizard, with big beefy hands, broad shoulders, and an annoying, braying laugh.

But the appellation made sense when it came to being

sneaky and slimy, both of which Dennis assigned to Lloyd in spades.

No matter what Rosey might say, Dennis had *The Roadrunner* locked down tightly whenever Lloyd came skulking around. The only door open to him without Rosey's express permission was the bathroom.

And even that door might stick on occasion. Dennis was just going to have to get that fixed sometime. Really. (Jamaal never had that problem for some odd reason...)

Dennis tried not to listen to Rosey and Lloyd chatting that evening. Lloyd had brought an interesting blueberry wine for Rosey to try, though honestly, she didn't like alcohol that much. Dennis would at least give Lloyd credit that every time he came to visit he brought something new, as if he was trying to figure out what Rosey liked.

Instead of just *asking* her what to bring. Like Jamaal had done at the start.

Finally, though, Rosey mentioned Dennis's name, so he had an excuse to join the conversation (as well as try to subtly push Lloyd's buttons to see if Dennis could get him to leave early).

"Dennis and I have been following the latest in shielding technology closely," Rosey said.

Dennis noted with approval that she'd taken a few sips of the wine and set it to the side. Though he could analyze the contents, he'd never know what it tasted like. He didn't need to know. If Rosey wasn't gulping it down, it must not be very good.

"Did you see the latest paper from Rosenburg et al?" Lloyd asked.

"Yes," Dennis said, calling up the details. "I think it's an interesting theory to add more organics to the metal, to give the metal more porousness."

Rosey nodded. "I like that theory as well, that the shredding occurs because we're fracturing time when we slip into hyperspace. Therefore, having metal that's more flexible, as it were, might help."

"I can see by the gleam in your smile that you have something you want to try," Lloyd purred.

Dennis couldn't really roll his eyes, but if he could, he probably would have hurt something in response to that statement.

"Maybe," Rosey teased. "Have you ever considered using an Inconel alloy as part of your shielding?"

Lloyd paused for a moment, considering. "Isn't the application for that mostly heat-based?"

"True," Rosey admitted. "But it has that porousness that I think we might be looking for."

"Interesting application," Lloyd admitted. "And not what others are pursuing at this time."

Even Dennis could recognize that this was the dangerous moment, when Lloyd needed to be distracted from asking more questions, such as why Rosey had chosen that metal in particular.

"As I said," Rosey added hastily. "I was extrapolating from the latest theories on the shredding."

Lloyd nodded. "That's very astute." He gave her a big smile. Then he looked thoughtful, and named a few other alloys that Rosey should consider.

Soon, the pair of them were happily geeking out on the different properties of various metals and Dennis gave a sigh of relief.

Rosey had been right. Lloyd was easily distractable. He

might start asking questions later, but for now, Rosey had him snowed.

And Dennis would just ignore the fact that they eventually moved from discussing metals to much more personal interactions. Though only after Rosey had forwarded some of the metals she'd already collected to Lloyd's workshop, where he'd promised to start conducting some experiments for her.

While Dennis might not approve of Lloyd the lounge lizard, at least he'd proven himself useful.

For now.

TWENTY-FIVE

While Rosey had been to a few of the Allied World systems before, usually it had been for business, meeting with racers and their teams. Those get togethers always took place on space stations, not on planet surfaces.

She had seen some of the more extreme genetic modifications and cyber implants that people indulged in. Such as the person who, instead of hair, had actual snakes growing out of their scalp, like a modern-day Medusa. Or the man who had an incredibly muscular torso wider than most doors, supported by metal mechanical legs with knees that bent backwards, like a chicken.

That hadn't really prepared her for being on a planet like Herkules, where nearly *everyone* was modified in some way or another.

Rosey tried not to gape like the tourist she was, but honestly, she couldn't help it.

Why would you decide that you needed a mushroom-top for a head? The cat ears and eyes, as well as canine snouts weren't too bad, but every imaginable type of animal appeared to be represented just on this one street alone. Including the long-necked giraffe they'd just passed.

"Do people spend their entire life with a single look? Or do they get bored and change styles?" Rosey had asked as they continued their journey on foot.

Jamaal had taken them to one of the largest cities on the planet, Aulus, and they were currently in what Rosey judged to be the border between the nicer parts of the city and the dodgier side.

The sidewalk they walked along needed repair, the road had potholes, and at least a quarter of the buildings they passed were boarded up. Given the modifications that people were sporting, there was obviously money here, but was all of it being spent adding enhancements?

"Most just find a theme and stick with it," Jamaal said. "Why? You thinking about getting some racing stripes?"

"Naw. Wouldn't want to make you jealous. Just because I'd rock such a look and you wouldn't," Rosey said with a grin.

"Oh, please. I could rock any look you named," Jamaal said.

"Even that, uhm, jellyfish toupee, up ahead?" Rosey asked.

"Perhaps I need to reconsider my stand," Jamaal admitted.

The banter made Rosey feel better, more settled.

They finally came to a building that looked somewhat out of place, given the slightly rundown nature of the streets surrounding it. The lobby was brightly lit, done in white and gold marble. A large, imposing desk sat in the middle of it, with a security guard sitting behind a glass wall, screens surrounding him.

Jamaal walked right up to the desk. "We're here to see Oswald Benegan," he said. "We have an appointment."

The guard looked up. Rosey peered back at him, curious

about his eyes, which were obviously artificial, given the brilliant blue color and the fact that they were larger than normal.

What could he see with such eyes? Heart rate? Temperature? Were they some sort of metal detector?

However, the guard didn't say anything. Smirked at Jamaal.

What, did he have some sort of X-ray vision? Was Jamaal naked under those robes he constantly wore?

Then the guard nodded them back to the elevators at the end of the lobby. "Bank C," he said. "The lift will take you to the floor."

That made sense. If someone did manage to sneak past the guard, they wouldn't be able to get anywhere. Not without some sort of key or code. And maybe not even then.

It seemed to surprise Jamaal when the elevator started descending. "Oswald's changed his office," he said when Rosey threw him a look.

"Good? Bad?"

Jamaal gave his patented shrug. "We'll see," he said breezily.

Jamaal had warned Rosey about Oswald, that he had no idea what the inventor looked like these days. Hopefully, it wouldn't be too outlandish. Rosey found that while all those modifications looked interesting, the ones she'd seen so far hadn't seemed too practical.

The lift didn't descend for too long—maybe five or six floors. When the elevator doors opened, they were facing yet another guard, sitting behind another protected desk, in front of a pair of dark brown doors.

This actually made Rosey feel better. She and Jamaal had discussed the necessity of leaving both the data chip as well as the circuit board with Oswald for a few days. Jamaal trusted Oswald, and that had to be good enough for her, since he'd allowed her to move the metallurgy experiments forward with

Lloyd. This meant they'd be on the planet for a few more days. Rosey planned on doing some sightseeing, visiting the famous rebuilt acropolis as well as the wells of Delphi.

This guard wanted to see some ID, which the first one hadn't asked about. Then again, whatever enhancements this goon had weren't as obvious. He was big, though. Taller than Jamaal, and maybe twice as wide.

It was only after he stood up that Rosey realized that his arms had been elongated, probably five inches past Human norm. He'd be a hell of a fighter, with incredible reach.

Until you adjusted to that and came in close, as the elbow was also moved out.

Had he originally been shorter? Rosey couldn't tell if his legs had been extended.

She might have to find a dojo around here, just to see what it was like to fight someone enhanced.

The guard left his desk and approached them with a hand scanner. Rosey wasn't sure what it measured, but it probably looked for weapons as well as recorded bio-markers.

Only after the scan was complete did the guard press a button on his desk. The dark doors behind him opened up into a brightly lit laboratory, a room roughly twenty feet square. The smells of bleach and heated metal were universal, but everything else was slightly askew. Rosey felt as if this was another type of hyperspace, with everything shifted off to one side, and she perceived everything at a slightly different angle.

The first room had at least a dozen long white tables covered with various electronic devices in different states of disassembly.

However, the monitors attached to some of the parts were moving. It took Rosey a few moments to realize she was actually watching little robots with big screen heads working on the various devices laid here. While some of the robot monitor heads were displaying white eyes and noses on the black screens, others were just running lines and lines of colorful code.

In addition, instead of a hard vinyl or tile floor, the surface was soft and spongy, like walking on thick gray rubber.

Jamaal led the way between the tables, heading toward the back of the room.

Rosey finally realized that the back wall was something of an illusion. It wasn't solid and covered in frosted-glass cupboards, which was what she'd thought from the front door. No, it was like a curtain, or a theatre scrim, that grew opaquely white as they approached, then shimmered and resolved into a transparent screen.

Behind the curtain sat the fattest man Rosey had ever laid eyes on. He was as nearly as wide as his desk. How much did he weight? 500 pounds? 600? If he could walk, it would only be with mechanical aid. His white face looked as though it had melted, going from the point of his scalp to his broad, thickly rolled neck. Brown hair, parted to the side, lay on top of that, looking like a wig. Piercing blue eyes peered out between the rolls of fat. Thick lips were curved in a sneer that quickly changed to an insincere smile. His chins wobbled as he nodded his greeting.

"Jamaal! Nice to see you. And you brought your partner in crime with you," he said. His voice was surprisingly soft and high for someone so large.

Two chairs rolled up from the side of the room, moving on their own.

It was a little creepy.

"I'm Rosey," she said as she followed Jamaal's example and took a seat.

The desk in front of Oswald was covered with wires, circuit boards, and tools. There was even an expensive welding apparatus to the side, though the barrel-like body had been enlarged, probably so that Oswald could wield it with his chubby fingers.

"I'm Oswald. Welcome to my domain," he said.

Rosey peered at him, but she didn't see any obvious enhancements.

Then a spider crawled up from under the collar of Oswald's white-and-blue-striped long-sleeved shirt. It obviously wasn't biological, as it was shiny and metallic, maybe an inch across with all its legs spread out. It crawled up along Oswald's neck, pausing for a moment to inject something, then slipped under one of the folds of his chin and back down the other side.

Rosey found herself sitting very still in her seat.

When Jamaal had said that Oswald had been enhanced, she'd assumed the obvious genetic engineering and cyberwear. Which she might see if he stood up, as she assumed his natural legs couldn't support his weight.

No, Oswald appeared to be *chemically* enhanced, with a constant supply of various compounds being delivered by a raft of AI-controlled spiders.

Rosey had read about such things but had never met someone like that before. They were only marginally sane, at least according to the news. Their chemical balance was so precarious that it took very little to nudge them into homicide or suicide.

Did Jamaal even know what he was getting into?

Then again, he'd supposedly worked with this Oswald for years. Maybe the inventor had always had the spiders, and so had perfected the fine tuning of his system.

Rosey realized that Jamaal had asked her a question and was looking at her with concern.

"Sorry," Rosey said after a moment. "Just wool gathering. Old age."

At the sneer Oswald gave her, Rosey knew she'd guessed right.

Oswald, for all his corpulent appearance, planned on living forever.

"What did you ask me?" Rosey said, turning to Jamaal.

"I'd like for you to show Oswald the board, first," Jamaal said.

A bright yellow bucket, the kind used by children at the beach, carried by a tiny robot, made its way to Rosey's side.

She slowly reached under her blue blouse, pulling out the modified traveler's purse she wore there. The cord holding it was made of spidersilk, impervious to most knives. She'd stored the circuit board in the purse, wrapped so tightly even she had difficulty tugging it free. She put it into the bucket and watched the tiny robot trundle away, going through what appeared to be a doggy door at the bottom of the screen, close to the wall on her left.

The robot must have a way to climb up the side of Oswald's desk, because Rosey saw the top of the bucket appear over the edge of it first, followed by the full bucket, then the little robot.

Only when Oswald reached into the bucket did Rosey notice that his fingers weren't all flesh. The first two on both hands were metal and contained sensors, or at least she supposed they did, as he ran then across the board, his eyes staring off in the distance.

"Interesting," he said, finally looking at Jamaal. "The board is uniquely constructed. I've never encountered such a combination of metals and plastic." He peered closely at it, his attention focused on the alien writing.

"Where did you find this?" Oswald said. His entire demeanor had changed. Instead of being laid back and sardonic, his body had grown tense, his tone full of wonder.

Jamaal glanced at Rosey, and she nodded.

Though she didn't like it, she understood the need to tell Oswald exactly what they were dealing with.

"From a wreck found in the outer reaches," Jamaal said.

"Where's the rest of the wreck?" Oswald asked. Though he sounded curious, he never took his eyes off the circuit board he held.

"Some moron blew it up," Jamaal admitted.

Rosey shook her head. It really was a travesty.

Reluctantly, Oswald put the piece to the side. "You said you salvaged something else from the wreck?"

Rosey nodded and stuck her hand down her shirt. She'd been storing the data chip in her bra. It would never fall out from there, and no one was good enough to be able to steal it from there.

She wiped it off on her pants before putting it into the bright red bucket that a little robot trundled over to her. (Though really, what was a little boob sweat when shared among friends?)

Oswald continued to study the circuit in front of him, though he was quivering with excitement.

"Ooooh," he said appreciatively when the little robot finally brought the bucket up to the desk.

That made Rosey smile. If nothing else, Oswald appreciated the piece they were handing him.

He turned it over in his hands, unerringly finding the data ports on one end and running his fingers across them.

"You think this is a data chip?" he asked, finally looking up.

"Yes," Rosey answered. "I believe it came from the black box on the ship. The data and cockpit recorder."

Oswald's eyes grew wide at that. Three spiders crawled out of his shirt and injected him with something before slinking away again.

"Wow," he finally said.

Rosey nodded. Wow, indeed.

"You need me to build something that can read this chip?" Oswald said, turning it over in his hands, glancing from Jamaal to Rosey and back again.

"Yes," Jamaal said. "I just need a basic phonetic transcript. The words will all be alien, so there's no way to know what's actually being said."

Oswald nodded. He looked thoughtful for a moment, then picked up the circuit board and dropped it into the little yellow bucket. The robot carrying it immediately started the long climb back down the desk.

"I've changed my mind. About my fee," he said, his eyes boring directly into Jamaal.

"Oh?" Jamaal asked. He seemed coiled, not laid back, as if he was going to spring into action or something equally ridiculous.

Didn't he understand the nature of the screen in front of them? He couldn't break through that—not even the goon outside the door could. It was probably impervious to bullets as well as lasers.

"I don't want your credits," Oswald said.

The little robot with the circuit board appeared next to Rosey, helpfully lifting up the bucket. She reached into it and pulled out the board, stowing it away again in her travel purse.

"I want that board as my payment," Oswald said.

Rosey opened her mouth to protest, then closed it again.

If she had the data chip, and a reader for it, telling her what was on it, did she really need the board anymore? It was an interesting artifact, but it didn't contain any data that was important.

Or did it?

She turned to Jamaal, who looked at her, then gestured with an open hand that the decision was hers.

She *was* the supposed expert here. At least with all things electronic and mechanical. And the board was still rightfully her possession.

"Fine," Rosey said grudgingly. "But I want to read your reports, learn what you discover about the board."

"That's more than agreeable," Oswald said. He gave her what looked like a sincere smile. "I look forward to discussing my findings with you."

Then Oswald turned his attention from them back to the data chip in his hands. He kept turning it over and over again, as if seeking something that kept sliding away from the surface.

Abruptly, the screen in front of them turned opaque, and they could no longer see Oswald at all.

"I think we should leave now," Jamaal said, standing.

"How will we know when he's finished?" Rosey said, still unsettled.

"He'll contact us," Jamaal said as he wound his way back through the tables and toward the rear door. "It doesn't make any sense for us to reach out to him before then. He'll be neck deep in his work, not eating or sleeping for days. What I've seen in the past is that he builds up huge fat reserves, then lives off them once he starts a project. He hasn't been working on anything for a while," Jamaal explained.

"Oh," Rosey said. The lift was waiting for them, and they rose silently back up to the lobby.

"You're sure we can trust him?" Rosey had to ask one last time as they made their way out to the street.

"I think we can, yes," Jamaal said.

Rosey nodded. She didn't like it. Oswald was...unsettling.

Hopefully, they hadn't just made a huge mistake.

TWENTY-SIX

Moe worried the entire trip down to Psykee. Was he doing the right thing, leaving Jun behind on *Aisha*? What would she think about the message he left for her?

Would she forgive him? Ever?

Atilio stayed strangely quiet on the trip down, as if he, too, was having second thoughts. It wasn't until they'd landed the flitter in Constantine's private spaceport that he finally looked at Moe and said, "It's going to be all right."

"Of course it will be," Moe said, trying to reassure both of them.

Moe didn't start to worry about what was immediately ahead of them until they were issued into Constantine's private study.

Dealing with Constantine.

Like many people in the Allied Worlds, Constantine had been genetically modified. He didn't go for any of the obvious cyberwear or modifications. No, his transformation was more subtle than that.

Sort of.

Constantine had perfectly symmetrical features, a proud Roman nose, and dark, piercing eyes. His skin color was darker than Atilio's, but lighter than Moe's—the ideal olive color, with brown undertones instead of pink. He wore his black curly hair in beautiful ringlets that looked extremely masculine. A little over six foot, four inches tall, with a deep, commanding voice, he presented an imposing figure. He kept his nails impeccably trimmed and polished, just like the white toga he wore, with gold and black trim around all the edges.

It took Moe a while to realize that Constantine looked exactly like someone's idea of a Greek god. If you weren't careful, you found yourself wanting to please him, just because his smile was so arresting, a moment of quiet perfection when he beamed at you.

Moe had yet to witness Constantine in anger. He assumed that state was just as impressive.

The marble floor of the study was done in shades of brown and gold, giving the hard surface a warm look. Real books lined the shelves—philosophy, physics, even poetry—a classical library in every sense of the word. A softly glowing globe filled the ceiling, giving off the precise right amount of light at every moment, automatically adjusting itself based on the sunlight streaming through the open windows.

On one wall stood a working fireplace, the marble of the mantle matching the floor, though not precisely the same. Constantine stood poised beside it when Moe and Atilio came in, followed by the three goons.

"Greeting distant travelers!" Constantine said, his smile ready and so happy.

Moe immediately felt better.

Then he reminded himself to count to three. In Tamil.

That took him out of his emotional state and back to an

intellectual one, so that Constantine's smile wouldn't completely dazzle him.

It was a trick that Atilio had taught him, and he was more than grateful for it.

"Greetings," Moe said after counting.

He wasn't sure what he was supposed to do next. He wasn't about to inquire after Constantine's health. The man was always going to be ridiculously healthy, given his modifications and access to medicines.

"I take it you were successful in your journey?" Constantine said. He continued to smile, though he turned down the wattage slightly.

Interesting. Had he expected something more from Moe, that Moe hadn't delivered?

"It was," Moe said. "The cargo was right where you said it was. We loaded it up with no problem."

He'd gone over the statements he would make to Constantine a few times in his head before their meeting, just to make sure that he didn't lie to the man.

Constantine could catch a lie as well as any god, judging men's souls.

"Good, good," Constantine said. He chuckled and shook his head. "Then I'm sure you'll have no problem staying here and enjoying my hospitality while I examine the catch, will you?"

"How long?" Moe asked. He didn't want to be down here too long. Jun was still aboard *Aisha*. He didn't want to leave her alone.

"Just a few days," Constantine said. "These products must be treated with care. Plus, once I see them, it will take a bit of time to find the perfect buyer. Which means that *your* portion of the proceeds may increase. Significantly."

Moe looked at Atilio, who shrugged. Moe could just about hear the words Atilio was thinking: *You're the boss.*

More credits would be good. Constantine was already supposed to pay them an exorbitant amount. Pausing here for a few days on Constantine's estate, being waited on hand and foot, and getting more credits than originally promised at the end?

Win-win, right?

Maybe Moe's luck was getting better.

"We'll wait for three days," Moe said. "Then, I'll have to insist that the contract be executed and we go on our way."

"I see," Constantine said. A slight testy note entered his voice.

Moe braced himself, but the storm cloud passed abruptly.

"Come, then, let us feast and toast to each other of the success of your mission!" Constantine said. He clapped his hands and servants bearing a huge amphora of wine along with a tray full of cups came in. They were all female, of course, scantily clad in short togas with their breasts exposed.

Atilio gave Moe a huge grin, while Moe himself merely smiled and took a glass.

He had something much better waiting for him in *Aisha*.

He hoped.

Constantine called Moe and Atilio back to his study in the afternoon of the second day. Moe was feeling pretty relaxed at this point, stuffed with good food and fully rested after a night on a bed that was surely illegal given how comfortable it had felt.

However, all those good feelings drained away immediately when he entered the study and saw Jun standing there.

She looked more angry than anything else, which was a good thing. Better angry than scared. Her hands were bound behind her and a gag was tied across her mouth. Her black hair was mussed, the ponytail askew.

And Sano was missing from around her neck.

"I have to say," Constantine said as Moe and Atilio drew closer, "I'm disappointed in you, Moe."

The frown Constantine directed at Moe felt like a physical blow. Moe shivered and clenched his fists, driving his nails into his palms while counting quickly in Tamil.

"Why is that?" Moe said slowly, still reeling from the double shock of seeing Jun as well as Constantine's emotional force.

"You left the greatest prize aboard your ship," Constantine said. "As specified in the contract, *anything* you found on the planet belongs to me."

"That doesn't apply to people!" Moe protested.

"Yes it does, actually," Constantine purred. The look of avarice that crossed his face was like yet another blow.

Moe was unprepared for the utter revulsion that suffused him in reaction to Constantine.

He knew that he wasn't able to hide his reaction, though, particularly based on the smirk Constantine threw him.

"The contract is executed here, on Psykee, where the owning and selling of any intelligent life form is entire legal," Constantine continued.

Moe rocked back on his heels. He hadn't expected that at all.

"Your princess here is going to fetch such a high price at the slave markets," Constantine continued.

Moe felt all the blood draining from his face. "You aren't going to ransom her?" he said, his words coming out in a harsh whisper.

"No," Constantine said with an elegant wave of his hand. "What's the fun in that? I'll gain much more by keeping her here. Credits in power and good will, not just money," he added.

Jun split her glare between Constantine and Moe.

"I'll buy her," Moe said, his voice cracking.

"You? What do you have to offer me?" Constantine said. That look of avarice was back in his eyes.

Moe couldn't help but shiver as he felt himself being assessed, like a butcher contemplating a fine cut of beef.

"*Aisha*," Moe said. "My ship." *My soul* he nearly added, though that might be too much.

"That piece of junk?" Constantine said.

"She means everything to me," Moe said, no longer looking at Constantine but directly at Jun. "It isn't the credits. Those mean nothing to you. You'd cut me to the quick, taking her. It's the best form of emotional torture, which is what you want, isn't it?"

Jun's eyes took on a thoughtful appearance.

Yes, Moe was giving away his only chance of escaping a world of servitude.

It was the only thing he had of value to give to Jun.

Either that, or his life. Though giving away *Aisha* was about the same.

Finally, Moe risked looking away from Jun and back at Constantine.

He had a thoughtful look on his face, his brow slightly furrowed in concentration.

"The princess means that much to you?"

"Yes," Moe breathed out, the word coming from the depths of his very soul.

"I don't know why I'm doing this," Constantine complained, "but the thought of you throwing away your life heedlessly after a princess who probably won't even deign to let you lick her shoes is delightfully ridiculous. She is yours."

Moe shuddered, the relief almost making him stagger.

"Thank you," he said. And he meant it.

"Now, the three of you need to leave, before I reconsider my generosity," Constantine said. "The gods have always been fickle that way."

Atilio was already in motion. He'd stepped forward, putting his arm across Jun's shoulders and began rushing them out of the room.

"Thank you," Moe said again, pausing at the door and looking back.

Constantine motioned for Moe to leave, though he didn't look at him, but continued to stare out the window, that thoughtful look still in place.

Moe hurried after the other two. Atilio kept his arm over Jun's shoulder protectively, like a policeman rescuing a captive. He led them unerringly toward the front door, which surprised Moe. He wouldn't have known the way. Evidently Atilio had mapped out the castle and planned an escape route.

Something which Moe should have done, but had never thought of.

It wasn't until after they'd left the building that Atilio finally tugged the gag from Jun's mouth.

"You ridiculous man," were the first words out of her mouth as she looked back over her shoulders at Moe.

"Where's Sano?" Moe asked as he slid a knife out of his pocket and went to work on the ties that bound Jun's wrists.

"She's up on *Aisha*," Jun complained. "It's all right. They can sell her as a pretty bobble. There isn't any way they can activate her. I had wanted to rescue her, but..."

"I'm sorry," Moe said. He suspected he'd be saying that a lot.

"You're still ridiculous," Jun said, though the smile she gave him softened the words considerably.

Atilio gave a huge sigh. "Look, can you two make googly-eyes at each other later? We gotta get outta here. And off planet. Any ideas?"

"I just need to contact my people," Jun said. "Someone will be here directly."

"Good," Atilio said. "In the meanwhile, hustle, people."

He set off at a brisk pace, leading them directly back toward the city of Zeno. Fortunately, Constantine's estate wasn't that far outside of the city. They should be able to rent a flitter to get them back to the spaceport in the nearest suburb.

While Atilio led the way, Jun fell back a little and offered her hand to Moe.

Grinning, Moe took it.

Seemed that perhaps Jun was going to forgive him after all.

And that maybe his luck was getting better.

TWENTY-SEVEN

Duri got daily reports from the military search team reporting to her. Of the ten Bigfoot hunters she'd focused them on, only two were still worth pursuing after a few days' time: a woman named Syne McCormick who worked as a mob accountant in the Allied Worlds, and a male merchant named Jamaal Akintola.

The person who'd come into her bedroom had definitely been male, which made Duri more inclined to lean toward Jamaal. Except that the merchant was loud and flamboyant. Not the type to clandestinely slip into someone's home. Plus, according to the records she had, he hadn't left the space station *Lorenzo* for quite some time.

Which left Duri unprepared when General Carrick requested a meeting with her, insisting that she come to his office instead of being friendly and just dropping by.

The general's office was about the same size as Duri's, rather small, with an impressively large desk pushed against the far wall, visitor chairs on the other side, and a two-drawer filing cabinet.

That was where the similarities ended.

The furniture in the general's office was all hard and utilitarian, including his own office chair. Nothing was suitable to hang on his walls, except a small flag representing the Kollective, which was bright red with the silhouette of a group of planets done in a curving design.

There were no pictures here. No stand by the door to hold coats or umbrellas. No tea-making paraphernalia or fridge for snacks. Even the floor was plain wood, no rugs to muffle the sounds of heels or boots clicking across.

The general himself fit the room. The only thing that might be considered soft about him was his skin color, which was a rich taupe with gold undertones, showing his Arabic heritage, as did his name, Abdul Harim Carrick, though she knew that he let his friends call him Abe. He kept his hair buzzed short, and as he'd never bothered dying it, silver now fringed the edges and was making headway across the center. His nose had obviously been broken as a young man, and he'd never had it fixed. It perched below dark, piercing eyes and above thin, disapproving lips. He wore a uniform, of course. Duri had never seen him in casual clothes.

As Duri wasn't certain of the reason for this meeting, she didn't start off with calling him by his name, but rather, his rank.

"You wanted to see me, General?" she said as she slid into the visitor chair he indicated.

She had no doubt that the chair was wired to a detection device, able to measure her heart rate and skin flush, despite how utilitarian it looked. And that their conversation would be recorded.

"What is your interest in Jamaal Akintola?" the general asked.

His desk held a few files, off to one side. The general now pulled the top one toward him.

Interesting. The edges of it were red, which meant that it was top secret.

"He's on the list of people who might have broken into my house to steal the reports on the alien wreck," Duri said. She knew that the military team she directed was already reporting to the general, so she wasn't certain why he needed to hear it from her as well. "Plus, he has the means to mount an attack. And he's been serious about finding the aliens for years."

The general nodded, then pushed the file across the desk to her.

When Duri looked up, he nodded, giving her permission to open it and look at the contents.

Duri couldn't help her gasp.

"He's a special agent for the Empire?" she asked as she quickly scanned the single page in front of her.

"We suspect so," General Carrick said. "We don't know for certain. He's been remarkably efficient at keeping a low profile. He appears to have retired from active duty a few years ago, so our surveillance of him had been stepped down."

Duri shook her head. "Is it possible that he mounted the attack on the alien wreck?"

The general gave a grim nod. "We think so. All official records show that he hasn't left the space station *Lorenzo*. However, we have evidence of him having been here, on New Rome."

The general reached beside him and pulled over the second folder. This one had even higher clearance stamped on it, Top Top Secret, as it were.

Inside was a picture of the man Duri knew was Jamaal.

He was walking down a street in New Rome, one hand

raised as if hailing a cab, his familiar orange robe swirling at his feet as he briskly moved along.

It took Duri a moment to place the time and date.

This was taken while the attack had been occurring.

"Where was this taken?" Duri asked.

"A few blocks away from the spaceport," General Carrick told her, his eyes boring into hers. "Only a single block away from the attack."

"Could it be coincidence?" Duri said, musing, though she knew in her gut that it wasn't.

No, Jamaal had not only arranged the attack on the alien wreck, he'd been there, directing it. And had decided to destroy the ship.

Why?

"Possibly it's a coincidence," General Carrick said. "But doubtful."

Duri nodded. "Do you have any reports yet from New Arrakis? Who might have visited the military base holding the wreck before my team got there?"

"We do," the general said, nodding. He pulled the last folder over. It was not labeled as top secret.

At least, not yet.

Duri flipped it open, finding a picture of an older white woman with short silver hair and a sardonic smile.

"This came from the base on New Arrakis. She arrived just before your team did, and left just afterward," the general said.

"Who is she?"

"Rosey De Vries. A somewhat famous speedship racer, though she's now retired and just builds racers. She's also a known associate of Jamaal Akintola." The general sighed. "The security on the storage facility at New Arrakis is, quite frankly, sub-par. Then again, they never expected to be holding anything of serious value. This Rosey presented false credentials that passed muster initially, though after doing more digging, were proven to be false."

"I see," Jun said. And she did.

While Jamaal was here, on New Rome, Rosey had been busy on New Arrakis.

What had she found?

"We weren't monitoring her comm, before," the general admitted. "We are now."

Jun nodded, knowing that it was a little late. This Rosey would surely be more careful now that she had the attention of the Kollective.

"Whatever you find on Jamaal, you need to bring to my attention immediately," the general said, obviously finishing up with their meeting as he grabbed back all the folders, closed them, and set them on the side of his desk again. "Do not, and I repeat, *do not* go after Jamaal on your own. He's extremely dangerous. Plus, there may be political ramifications."

"I will be sure to let you know," Duri promised.

It was an easy promise to make.

Back in her own comfortable domain, Duri had Kiley make her a cup of tea while she meditated, just breathing in and out, watching the dust motes dance in the sunlight streaming thru her tall windows.

Only after she'd taken a few sips did she find her mind slipping back onto the trail, her next victim in her sights.

She barely heeded the alert that beeped at her, telling her that the *exact* combination of metals and alloys that had composed the majority of the alien ship had been purchased, other than to note that the delivery address was De Vries Industries, Inc.

No, Duri wasn't going after Jamaal. He was likely to be too

dangerous. She remembered that moment when he seemed about to pounce on her.

If he was a trained agent, he'd probably been considering whether or not to kill her.

However, this Rosey. She was his weak link. She wasn't trained in espionage. Plus, the Emperor wasn't about to protect her. She was merely a civilian.

Exposed. In the open. A viable target.

And one that Duri had just set her sights on.

TWENTY-EIGHT

Jamaal spent the morning of day after the meeting with Oswald criticizing the new acropolis on Herkules, snarking with Dennis about how the *feng shui* was all wrong.

"It should be all about the hard and soft," Dennis was saying. "These idiots thought that all *hard* was the way to go. As if that would be more impressive."

"Well, they were trying to be authentic," Rosey said.

And they had been. Kind of.

The left half of the acropolis was an exact replica of the ruins that remained on Earth, complete with the moss growing up through the stone on the footpath as well as the blast marks on half of the columns, where a stupid terrorist attack had occurred just as Humanity had discovered hyperspace.

The right half was pristine, and looked like how the acropolis might have appeared when it had first been built, the columns done in outrageous colors, the statues all bearing Human-colored faces.

Jamaal jumped slightly when his comm buzzed.

It was an unknown caller.

Interesting, since no one except Rosey and Harkeen had this number.

Was Oswald already finished? It had been only a day.

Even though it was an unknown number, Jamaal still answered it.

"This is Emma," came the surprising response.

"Really?" Jamaal said, shocked into standing still. He found himself coming to attention, though he'd never been in the military.

Not really. Though he could impersonate a general more believably than most.

She quoted his old call signal at him, something that only she and maybe a handful of others possibly knew.

"You have my attention," was all that Jamaal would commit to.

It probably was Emma and not someone impersonating her. However, he wouldn't trust an open line. Not like this.

How was she contacting him, anyway? Was she in the system? Humanity had no ansible. This had to be a recording, not a live discussion.

"We have a report of Princess Jun on the planet Psykee, which is less than an hour's travel from your current location," Emma said. "In the city of Zeno. We can give you better coordinates once you arrive."

"I see," Jamaal said. He was but wasn't surprised that Emma would reach out to him.

Though he was retired, he'd always been trustworthy. And Emma knew him well. Or at least had, at one point.

"You are the closest operative," Emma said in response, confirming Jamaal's assessment. "We just need you to confirm her presence. Can you do it?"

That she was asking and not ordering Jamaal confused

him. Of course, if Emma, and the Empire, called, he'd jump back into action.

Or at least, this time he would.

Seemed that it wouldn't take a lot to get him back into the game.

Then he remembered that Princess Jun was something of a xenolinguist.

This could all work out in his favor.

"Yes," he said. "We'll be there in under two hours."

Rosey raised her eyebrows at that, making no effort not to listen in.

"We have to go," Jamaal said. "Dennis? Get ready to depart. We're heading off planet."

"We're what?" Rosey said.

Jamaal took a few steps out of the crowds before he realized that she wasn't following him.

"What do you mean we're leaving? What about Oswald?" Rosey said. She stood stock still, her arms crossed over her chest, glaring at him.

"I'll explain once we're on our way," Jamaal said, though he didn't really have any idea what story he was going to tell her.

He couldn't tell her that his former handler when he'd been an assassin for the Emperor had just asked him to do her a favor, now, could he?

Rosey merely glared at him, her expression closed off.

"Fine," she said after a few moments, trudging up to him. "But this explanation had better be a good one."

"It will be," Jamaal promised.

At least she didn't ask anything else as they made their way quickly back to the spaceport, giving him time to come up with something good. Or so he hoped.

"Xenolinguist, eh?" Rosey asked after Dennis had gotten them into hyperspace.

It was only a short jump between the two planets, less than fifteen minutes time. The actual journey wasn't what would take the two hours—it was getting on and off planet, as well as to an area where hyperspace travel was acceptable in terms of space traffic.

No one wanted a ship popping up out of nowhere and possibly damaging or flying into another ship. Most planets had a wide circle around them that clear before their hyperspace zone began. Spaceships weren't supposed to fly into hyperspace—or, more importantly, arrive from hyperspace—anywhere other than in this area.

"Yes," Jamaal said. He almost wished that they'd be in hyperspace for a longer period of time, so he could use Rosey's workout room. He'd always found going through one of the more flowing forms of Tai Chi settled him when he was in hyperspace, letting him find his body again, so that he could operate as well in this skewed space as in regular space.

"She's gone missing," Jamaal said. "And her family is very important. I received notification of where she is."

Hopefully, he'd be able to rescue her on his own, without the need for calling in any support.

Emma had said in her initial message to only report on the princess's whereabout, to leave it to the Empire to mount the rescue.

Jamaal wasn't in the habit of disobeying directives.

Then again, he was retired, wasn't he?

"Why you?" Rosey said, her eyes narrowed, watching him closely.

"You know how it is," Jamaal said breezily. "Friend of a friend. And I owe the family a favor."

Rosey shook her head. Before she could say anything more, he quickly added, "I seem to have the gift of gab. The family believes I can talk my way in and out of any situation."

Jamaal gave Rosey a toothy grin.

Though Rosey didn't look as though she believed Jamaal, she still only rolled her eyes at him and didn't direct Dennis to turn right back around and go to Herkules.

At least for now.

They reinserted back into real space without a hitch. Once they were in orbit around the planet, Jamaal reached back out to Emma, on the number she'd called him at.

Didn't get a response, as he'd anticipated. How she'd gotten through to him on Herkules was another matter.

His comm buzzed a few moments later. No message. Just coordinates.

Jamaal fed them to Dennis, who informed the pair of them that it was a neighborhood café in a suburb of the city of Zeno.

Huh. So maybe not a hostile kidnapping situation at all.

Was it possible that the princess had run away? That she hadn't been kidnapped?

That seemed to be the most likely explanation at this point.

Hopefully, she wouldn't be too much of a pain to work with, once they had the alien transcription from Oswald.

Jamaal and Rosey quickly took a flitter down to the planet, then hopped into a taxi.

The neighborhood the taxi dropped them off in was on the outskirts of the city itself. Sleepy little place, with wide lanes for trucks making deliveries. The buildings along the main street were all two stories, with large storefronts on the first floor and flats on the second. The shops were the usual mix of used-clothing boutiques, insurance agencies, cafés, tattoo parlors, instant body modifications, restaurants and such.

Jamaal checked his comm to make sure that he had the correct location before he pushed the door to the café open. Tall wooden booths lined the two long walls going back into the room. On the right, under the broad windows, sat little tables. An older man sat there, palish skin and curly hair, keeping a sharp eye out on the street, the door, as well as the occupants.

Some sort of informant? Jamaal made a mental note about him before he moved further into the café.

In the last booth on the left sat the princess, with her back to the door. She was drinking a cup of something and having a friendly chat with a dark-skinned young man with straight black hair.

Not a hostile kidnapping at all.

Huh.

Jamaal walked breezily up to the table and sat down in the booth next to the man, while Rosey did the same, sitting beside the princess.

"Who are you? Why are you here?" the man asked.

Before the man could do something stupid like reach for the laser he still had strapped to his hip (and was not trained in its use *at all*), Jamaal said, "Hello Princess. We're here to rescue you."

The eyeroll Jamaal received in response to that was truly impressive.

"I don't need rescuing," Princess Jun said primly.

Interesting. The man held up a hand, telling the informant sitting close to the door to stay seated, that it was okay.

For now.

Rosey was giving Jamaal an appraising look.

"A princess?" she asked archly.

"Princess Jun Ogawa, meet Rosey De Vries, racer extraordinaire," Jamaal said with an open gesture.

The two women gave each other an appraising look, then nodded.

"Do you want to introduce us to your kidnapper?" Jamaal said, turning to look at the man sitting next to him.

"This is Mohammed Abdul Nuwan Pradeep Aruna Tennakoon Herath," Princess Jun said proudly. "A freighter captain who has already performed what *rescue* needed doing."

"Just call me Moe," the man broke in.

The princess gave him a quick smile before turning a frown back at Jamaal. "And you are?"

"Jamaal Akintola," he said, bowing his head. "At your service."

"As I've mentioned before, I don't need any rescuing," Princess Jun said. "Though I am curious how you found me."

Jamaal shrugged. "Friend of a friend supplied me with your exact coordinates."

Before either the princess—or worse, Rosey—could start questioning Jamaal, the lookout came striding toward their table.

"We got incoming, boss," he said. "Local authorities." He reached up and touched his ear, indicating that he'd been listening to radio chatter. "We gotta go."

"Just a second," Jamaal said. He quickly pulled out a scanner from his robes and directed it at the Moe, Princess Jun, and the other man.

"Did you know that you have half a dozen trackers inserted into your clothing?" he asked the princess casually.

"What? No. How?"

"Constantine," Moe said grimly. "Local crime lord," he added as explanation.

So it seemed the princess had actually needed rescuing, and that this Moe had done it.

"Good. So consider yourself rescued a second time," Jamaal said as he stood. Rosey was already striding out the door. "Once we leave this area, I may have a job proposition for you."

"A job?" Princess Jun said as she scooted out.

"Yes," Jamaal said. "We might have access to a new alien language that needs to be deciphered."

He knew he was taking a risk mentioning it in public.

However, he also knew that from the glowing look of excitement on the princess's face that she'd take the bait.

Now, they just had to get out of here in one piece.

TWENTY-NINE

Rosey was already on the comm with Dennis. "We need to get out of here. Fast. What's the closest escape vehicle you can find?"

The man she hadn't yet been introduced to kept up with her as they hit the street. He was slightly shorter than she was, a little on the pudgy side, with curly hair and a rueful smile.

"Who you talking with?" he asked as he scanned the street.

"My ship, in orbit," Rosey said.

"Turn right, then right again," came Dennis's response.

The man jogged in front of her as they went.

Huh. He was in better shape than she would have assumed.

Cute butt, though she did tend to like them taller.

As soon as they turned the corner, Rosey's eyes were drawn to the bright-red muscle car that was parked just up the block. Two-door, low to the ground, with fatter tires than she'd use but might give the vehicle a good grip.

"What, this mid-life crisis machine?" Rosey asked Dennis.

"Fastest thing around here," Dennis assured her.

205

"Fine, what are the codes?" Rosey said as she approached the driver side.

"Surely you don't expect me to aid your juvenile delinquency?" Dennis asked in mock horror.

"Dennis," Rosey growled.

The man she was with gave her a quick grin. "Mouthy," he commented.

Rosey shrugged. "He has his merits."

That just got her a bigger grin. Particularly as the two doors to the muscle car swung open.

Jamaal, Moe, and the princess came hustling up. Moe and the princess got in one side, into the tiny backseat. Jamaal elegantly folded himself up on the other side.

"Hey, new guy. Got a name?" Rosey asked as she slid into the driver's seat.

"Atilio Perez," he said. "At your service."

Rosey was pleased that he hadn't automatically assumed that he could drive this beast better than she could.

"Fastest route out of here," Rosey told Dennis as the car revved up.

Oh jeez. The owner had added a fart can to the engine, making it three times louder than it needed to be.

Atilio made a rude noise. "They're going to be able to track us through the noise of that alone," he grumbled.

"Hopefully, they won't get a chance," Rosey said as she studied the map Dennis had laid out for her on the heads-up display.

"They're converging on the café," Atilio said, his voice lowered. "Someone tipped them off that there was a princess on the loose, and that there might be a reward offered by the family for her return."

"Constantine," Moe said again, as if that was the full answer.

Rosey slid out of the parking spot and pulled a quick U-turn, not heading toward the main drag, in case that caught someone's attention.

Jamaal was using his scanner to identify the various trackers that had been inserted into Princess Jun's clothing. "Window, please," he said.

Atilio found the appropriate button and depressed it so that Jamaal could start tossing trackers out the window.

"They spotted us," Atilio warned.

Rosey saw the bright cherry-colored lights in her rearview mirror. "Let's see how this thing flies," she said as she increased the acceleration.

Fortunately, the beast had been tuned up recently. For all that it sounded like an ancient hog, it moved smoothly, and more importantly, quickly.

Those fat tires really did grip the road well, particularly as Rosey rammed them around a corner.

Not because she was trying to get away from the idiots following her.

No.

She'd needed to feel how the car responded as she started pushing its edges.

"You don't have a stretchsuit on," Dennis warned as Rosey took another turn at full speed.

Rosey just snorted. She also wasn't likely to need all the features one would provide, such as extra oxygen.

Though protection from the Gs they were going to be pulling might be nice, as she nudged the speedometer up.

Atilio nodded in appreciation as she took the next curve.

The others in the backseat grumbled at being tossed from side to side.

Too bad.

Rosey really needed to get them out of the local area. Then they'd split up, find new vehicles, and make their way to the spaceport.

"They're calling for backup," Atilio warned.

Crap.

Rosey turned and raced down two more blocks, heading toward the speedway, getting on at the first exit.

"You're going the wrong way!" came the response from both Atilio and Dennis.

"Duh," Rosey said as she sped down the exit ramp and directly into oncoming traffic.

Despite it being late afternoon, traffic was pretty light. She ignored the honking vehicles and continued speeding down the expressway, only having to swerve around idiots a few times.

None of the cops had followed her.

As they approached the next exit, Rosey jammed on the brakes, tires screeching satisfactorily, then sped up the exit ramp.

There wasn't a lot out here. Some sort of strip mall to the side, generic grocery store and and all-you-can-eat buffet.

Then she saw what she'd been looking for.

Car dealership.

"You see what I'm seeing?" she asked Dennis.

"Two blocks, take a left, then down to the end of the cul-de-sac," Dennis said. "I'll turn back on the car's tracking system once we've left orbit, so the owner can find it."

The cul-de-sac was surprisingly empty. New homes were being built at the end closest to it entrance. The back of it, where they dumped the car, was all woods.

After Rosey and the others exited, Jamaal took a few moments wiping down the interior, removing as many of the fingerprints as he could.

"Could you get Dennis to pop the hood, please?" Atilio asked.

Rosey did, curious what Atilio wanted to see.

The pair of them studied the engine for a few moments, before he pulled out a tiny pen-light laser and sent a beam through a box on the side.

"Tracker?" Moe asked.

"Naw," Atilio said with a grin. "Stupid fart can."

Rosey nodded with approval. This Atilio was much more than he seemed.

"Two or three cars?" Rosey asked as she led the way back up the street, toward the car dealership.

"Two," Jamaal replied. "One for the women. A second for the three men."

"You got it. Dennis?"

The sigh she received was truly impressive.

"Fine," he said, grumbling. "But I expect a higher decorating budget next month."

"Just make sure everything's ready and primed to go as soon as we get there," Rosey warned.

"But what about *Aisha*?" Princess Jun asked.

"Is there a second princess we need to rescue?" Rosey asked, though she didn't stop moving.

"*Aisha* is my ship," Moe said.

"We'll rescue her at some other time," Atilio reassured him.

Rosey was about to reply that perhaps they could use this *Aisha* for a getaway when a warning beep came through her comm.

It took Rosey a few moments to figure out what that sound meant.

Swearing, she pulled out the traveler's purse that she still wore under her blouse, then tugged out the circuit board.

"We are so stupid," Rosey said as she handed it to Jamaal.

He looked at it, then brought it up to peer more closely at it.

There was no alien writing on it. The board bore a striking similarity to the original. However, it wasn't the same.

Oswald had stolen the original.

And Rosey would bet that he'd taken the data chip too, that all she had was an imitation.

The warning message she'd received on her comm had been a notification that the ITT tag that she'd injected into the board had just pinged a system far from here.

Rosey glared at Jamaal, who appeared shocked.

They had no alien data chip. No alien circuit board. They'd been saddled with a princess, her boyfriend, and his second in command.

What were they going to do now?

"Come on," Atilio said. "Let's get out of here and figure out our next step."

Rosey nodded, falling into step beside Atilio.

Oswald had screwed them.

Good thing Rosey wasn't feeling overly vengeful.

Yet.

"No, we do *not* need to go to Ishiman first," Rosey fumed at Jamaal. "We need to head toward the opposite side of the galaxy, quite frankly. That's where Oswald is heading."

The five of them were seated around the table in the eating nook. Dennis had ohhed and ahhed over having an actual princess visit him, and had spent time pointing out all the decorations and improvements that he'd recently made to the ship, along with broad hints about what he could do with a superior budget. It had taken a bit to get him to shut up, though Rosey hadn't had to forbid him from talking to them.

Yet.

They were still in orbit around Psykee, despite the fact that Rosey had wanted to take off *immediately*.

"I need to deliver Princess Jun back to the court," Jamaal countered.

Serious Jamaal was there, just under the surface. Rosey was now pretty sure that his story about some "friend of a friend" calling in a favor was bullshit.

Jamaal had at one point worked for the Emperor. No idea what he'd done. He was too outlandish to be a spy or an ambassador. Perhaps, he'd been an informant. He did have that gift of gab, knew everyone, and had possibly placed the right information in the right ear at the right time.

"Princess Jun can take herself back, thank you very much," replied said princess coldly.

"No, you cannot," Jamaal countered before Moe could say anything, though given his emphatic nod, he seemed to agree.

"Princess, your family is worried about you," Jamaal said. "And your parents. You no longer have your governess. Plus, there's a local warlord who's put his sights on you. You must return to court, make sure that everyone knows you're alive and well. After that, you are a free woman and can do what you'd like. But you have a responsibility to the royal family first, and you know it."

Princess Jun made a face at that, but she stopped arguing.

"If you can help me get my ship away from Constantine, I can take Jun back to Ishiman," Moe interjected.

Rosey couldn't help but roll her eyes. "Right. Step into an argument with this local warlord? Why would I want to do that, again?"

Moe spread his hands wide across the table. "Because you have a good heart?"

Even Jamaal snorted at that.

"My heart's made of credits and gears," Rosey quipped.

Interesting. While Moe didn't seem to know what to do about that, it did appear to spark Atilio's interest.

"I'll pay you," Princess Jun said quietly.

Of course, the stupidly proud Moe said, "No."

"Look, how about this?" Rosey said, pausing as she thought through her plan. "Moe, you, me, and Atilio go after Oswald. You help me recover my stolen merchandise. While we're off doing that, Jamaal and the princess can go back to court. After the three of us deal with Oswald, I'll help you get your ship out of Constantine's clutches."

"And you do realize that when Rosey is offering you *her* help, what she means is that she'll sweet talk *me* into helping with your upcoming crimes," Dennis added.

Rosey tilted her head from side to side. Dennis wasn't completely wrong in that. She would need his expertise getting in and out of whatever shipyard contained this *Aisha*.

Moe and Atilio looked at each other. Atilio shrugged, obviously indicating that it was Moe's decision.

Moe slowly nodded. "All right. I can help you track down your stolen merchandise. But then I would really appreciate your help freeing *Aisha*."

Rosey didn't comment that if Constantine was as much of

a bully as he appeared to be, he'd probably slag the ship before they returned.

However, that was a problem for another day.

"How are we supposed to get to Ishiman?" Princess Jun asked.

"I'm certain that Jamaal has the necessary contacts," Rosey said, quirking one eyebrow his direction.

Jamaal nodded. "I do," he said. "There will be a military escort arriving in the next hour."

Rosey narrowed her eyes at Jamaal. He gave her a wide grin.

Yup. Informant. Higher connected to the court of the Emperor than Rosey had known.

However, she wasn't going to give him grief about that publicly. Certainly not in front of strangers.

It was bad enough that these people had to be taken into their confidence about the alien wreck.

"Be careful," Jamaal warned Rosey. Again. "Oswald can be dangerous. And there may be others involved who will be coming after you."

"Then you better get going on your errand," Rosey said. "We'll meet up with you back here, on Psykee."

Jamaal paused, but nodded. "We'll be back here as soon as we can be," he promised.

With that, Jamaal and Princess Jun left the table to go get ready. Moe excused himself, probably looking for a little something from his sweetheart.

"That leaves us old folks, here to save their asses. Again," Rosey said to Atilio.

"Who you calling old?" he teased. He paused, then added, "You got anything you need fixing? Something that needs tuning up before we head out?"

Rosey nearly blew him off, but then paused. Atilio had

been introduced as the second in command on *Aisha*. Was he the mechanic as well?

"What do you know about the latest research in starship shielding?" she had to ask.

"You mean the mixing of organics in with the metal?" Atilio asked.

Rosey smiled at him, and they were off, nerding out about the latest ship technology.

Maybe this trip to go confront Oswald wouldn't be all bad.

READ MORE!

Be sure to pick up all the books in the Live Alien Contact series.

Alien Wreck
Alien Codex
Alien Encounter
Alien War

Available at your favorite retailers!

ABOUT THE AUTHOR

Leah R Cutter writes page-turning fiction in exotic locations, such as a magical New Orleans, the ancient Orient, Hungary, the Oregon coast, rural Kentucky, Seattle, Minneapolis, and many others.

She writes literary, fantasy, mystery, science fiction, and horror fiction. Her short fiction has been published in magazines like *Alfred Hitchcock's Mystery Magazine* and *Talebones*, anthologies like Fiction River, and on the web. Her long fiction has been published both by New York publishers as well as small presses.

Find Leah's books on Knotted Road Press at (www.KnottedRoadPress.com)

Follow her blog at www.LeahCutter.com.

Reviews

It's true. Reviews help me sell more books. If you've enjoyed this story, please consider leaving a review of it on your favorite site.

Come someplace new...

Do you enjoy exploring strange new worlds, new cultures, new people?

Journey into the various lands envisioned by Leah R Cutter.

Sign up for my newsletter and I'll start you on your travels with a free copy of my book, *The Island Sampler.*

I will never spam you or use your email for nefarious purposes. You can also unsubscribe at any time.

http://www.LeahCutter.com/newsletter/

ABOUT KNOTTED ROAD PRESS

Knotted Road Press publishes dynamic fiction set in exotic locations. Our authors cover a wide range of genres including science fiction, fantasy, mystery, literary, and poetry. We also have unique non-fiction voices in genres such as autobiography, business, cookbooks, and how-tos. We offer both DRM-free ebooks and print books for a global readership.

Knotted Road Press
www.KnottedRoadPress.com

www.ingramcontent.com/pod-product-compliance
Lightning Source LLC
Chambersburg PA
CBHW060300100726
47907CB00002B/219